WITHDRAWN

Five hundred numbered copies and fifteen lettered copies of **MOONTOWN** have been printed.

This is copy
359

MOONTOWN
Peter Atkins

Also by Peter Atkins

**MORNINGSTAR
BIG THUNDER
WISHMASTER AND OTHER STORIES**

MOONTOWN
Peter Atkins

Earthling Publications / Halloween 2008

Moontown copyright © 2008 by Peter Atkins.
Dustjacket and tip sheet art copyright © 2008 by Alan M. Clark.
Dustjacket design by Deena Warner.
This limited edition and interior design copyright © 2008 by Paul Miller.

First edition, first printing
October 2008

ISBN-13: 978-0-9795054-5-4
ISBN: 0-9795054-5-3

Moontown is the fourth book in Earthling's Halloween Series.

EARTHLING PUBLICATIONS
P.O. Box 413
Northborough, MA 01532 USA
Email: earthlingpub@yahoo.com
Website: www.earthlingpub.com

Printed in the U.S.A.

*She raised her little eyebrow
At the Dark Thing which had followed her.
She said, "I'm only dreaming!"
"Dream this," it said. And swallowed her.*

—from "Jenny and the Dark"
by Wilfred Tibble

1

The abandoned garment factory was lit only by the shafts of moonlight that entered through its vast institutional-style windows, and everything inside was covered with the dust and grime of long neglect.

If Anthony Esposito had had the time and leisure to form an opinion, he'd've log-lined the place as a Victorian sweatshop dinosaur, derelict for decades.

But Anthony was forming no opinion. Anthony couldn't give a shit about the details or the history of the place.

Because Anthony was running for his life.

He wasn't very good at running for his life. He was forty years old and hadn't seen the inside of a gym since his last unreciprocated office crush. But he was doing the best he could, even though the pulse of his panting breath was pounding in his head like a death-metal kick-drum on overdrive. He was running desperately down the narrow central aisle between the huge industrial sewing machines that crowded the floor, trying to avoid the disused power cords coiled as if eager to trip him and the occasional spool-arm left extended out into the aisle from whenever the last whistle blew on the factory's long-ago last shift.

He risked a look back over his shoulder, past the massive bales of fabric piled along the walls, to where the workhouse was lost in a mosaic of shadow, a huge jagged-edged block of darkness that had completely swallowed the rear of the factory, wall to wall and floor to ceiling.

Peter Atkins

It was moving.

Anthony wasn't crazy. He was afraid but not fucking delusional. He wasn't imagining anything. The darkness was in motion. The darkness was in pursuit. And it was gaining on him.

A whimper escaped his mouth, unconscious and involuntary, a high-pitched plea of the kind he probably hadn't made since he left the cradle. There was nobody to hear or answer it, though: no mommy or daddy to switch on the light and rock him out of the nightmare. It was down to his lungs and his legs to save him, and he was frankly far from sure that they were up to the task.

There was a door at the far end of the towering machines. Not an exit but at least something to head for, something to get on the other side of, something to hide behind. Anthony raced towards it, passing bundles of rags and discards in which his peripheral vision caught fleeting and disturbing glimpses of things that looked like limbs, protruding from the rags and blue with death. As if sensing his sight of these things, a delighted giggle echoed out from the galloping darkness behind him.

Anthony reached the door, his panicked hands grappling clumsily with its handle, the old-fashioned faux-crystal knob slipping and sliding loosely around the pinion shaft. He glanced to his side. Propped up beneath one of the windows, all but lost in the shadows, were two life-size rag dolls.

They had to be rag dolls, right? Limbs splayed spastically and heads lolling loosely like that? They couldn't be children. Couldn't be dead children. But what doll manufacturer would make dolls with something so horribly wrong with their mouths?

Moontown

Pulling his eyes away from the looseness of their bodies, Anthony fumbled again with the doorknob, feeling the hungry darkness racing up the last few feet separating them. Finally, the pinion caught, the latch clicked, and the door opened. Anthony ran through it into the smaller room beyond, just seconds before the darkness obliterated the whole of the factory floor.

Slamming the door shut behind him, Anthony leaned back against it, gathering his breath for one precious dangerous moment before stepping further into the room. As he did so, a cloud moved away from the moon and the silver light revealed that Anthony was standing amongst seven dead children.

Anthony's body flooded with a wash of what, had he had the time for the luxury of self-delusion, he would have pretended was pity and sympathy but was actually fear and disgust—fear and disgust mollified only by his realization a second later that the figures sprawled around the room in various postures of death had never been alive at all. They were merely more examples of the disturbingly lifelike rag dolls.

Every doll's mouth had been stuffed—overstuffed—with rags and tatters, and their pink cotton cheeks were distended and bloated in vile representation of death by suffocation.

Turning to avoid the sight of them, Anthony found himself looking into a wall-mounted mirror and staring at his reflection.

Which wasn't his reflection at all.

Used to be, though. The figure in the mirror was Anthony at eight years old. Same hair color. Same eyes. Same distinctive mole pattern on his cheek.

But it wasn't a painting or a photograph. It was a reflection. A reflection that, impossibly or not, was mirroring Anthony's actions precisely—hands raising in alarm, mouth opening in uncomprehending shock.

And then the door flew open, slamming against the wall.

Anthony just had time to see the dread bloom on his mirrored child's face before he looked to the doorway. And there, emerging from the shadows like a nightmare to which the darkness had just given birth, was exactly who Anthony expected to see.

*

His screams brought his parents rushing into his bedroom, as they always did. Dad flooded the room with light from the wall-switch by the door while Mom ran and held him.

"Anthony, honey, it's okay," she said, while his eyes darted disbelievingly around the room to try and spot the monster's hiding place.

"Just another nightmare, son," Dad said from over by the door, but Anthony heard the disappointment in his voice and saw the judgment in his eyes. You should know better, *Dad was really saying,* You're a big boy now. *And Anthony was a big boy now. He'd be eight years old next birthday. He was ashamed and sad that Dad was angry at him, but he was more concerned with trying to make his throat work. He gasped and gulped, and Mom started rubbing gently at his neck.*

"Breathe, sweetie, breathe," she said. "Just relax. It's okay."

Dad had moved to Anthony's desk and was flicking through his pile of comic books, as if trying to find something to blame.

Anthony's chest heaved suddenly, and air rushed reassuringly into his lungs. Mom kissed his brow. "Good boy," she said, "that's better."

He looked past her to where Dad was screwing up Anthony's

MOONTOWN

carefully sorted collection, throwing a recent Spider-Man *among last year's run of* Justice League.

"*He's not* there, *Dad,*" Anthony said.

"*What?*" Dad said, turning to look at him.

"*He doesn't live there,*" Anthony said. "*He lives in the dark.*"

"*He doesn't live* anywhere,*" Dad said, an edge of irritation in his voice. "He's not* real, *Anthony. He doesn't exist. There's no such person as the Ragman.*"

*

The Ragman stood in the open doorway clad in the lunatic costume that Anthony had spent three decades trying to forget, a crazy quilt of a hundred different fabrics chaosed together in a nightmare motley like a clown dressed by a cubist. Bozo via Picasso. Koko courtesy of Braque. His black eyes were locked with insane delight on Anthony and his right hand was clenched eagerly around a bundle of rags, which he raised and shook slightly to be sure that Anthony knew what was coming.

"Anthony," he said. "There you are."

Not angry at all, really. More excited that the long game of hide-and-seek was finally over and the real fun could begin at last.

Anthony wanted desperately to look away, but he couldn't. Like a rabbit mesmerized by a snake, he didn't do anything at all, just stayed very still, hardly breathing, hardly thinking, hardly moving.

The Ragman moved, though. He moved with unbelievable swiftness. Moved like his feet weren't propelling him at all, like he was gliding effortlessly forward, albeit at breakneck speed.

His left hand gripped Anthony's face and throat, his long filthy fingers forcing the man's mouth open wide, and his right hand jetted forward, forcing the bundle of rags into Anthony's mouth, pushing them deep and mercilessly deeper.

Anthony tried to struggle, but this long-feared consummation filled him with paralyzing dread and left his body limp and helpless. *Just another rag doll*, he thought despairingly as the Ragman's ecstatic giggle echoed hideously in his head. He felt his traitorous throat close around the choking rags, felt his breath vanish, felt his frantic heart pump wildly—and then felt his loosely flailing hand suddenly grasped firmly by another's.

"Anthony! Come back!" said a female voice. It sounded strange, distant, sounded like it was coming from a different place, even as he felt the undeniable pressure of her hand, gripping his tightly, pulling him...

...jerking him forward in his folding chair.

He was still choking and gasping, but air was already flowing into his unencumbered throat.

There were no rags in his mouth.

There was no monster from his childhood.

There was nothing here to harm him.

He looked up, blinking in the morning sunlight that was shining into the group-study room, and saw that his hand was still held by the young woman sitting next to him.

"It's okay, Anthony," said Shelley Campbell. "You're back. We're back."

2

Doctor Alex Drayton watched as Shelley instinctively put a comforting arm around Anthony's shoulder and stared at the still-shaking man in a plainly sincere attempt at reassurance. It was both charming and professionally intriguing, Alex thought. Esposito had nearly twenty years on the girl, and yet her default impulse was not merely to soothe the troubled adult but to mother the frightened child within. Alex made a mental note to explore that issue with Shelley in their next private session.

Anthony, without yet saying anything to Shelley, took his eyes off her—*embarrassed at what she'd seen of his secrets*, Alex wondered, *or simply reorienting himself?*—and looked around the room, blinking himself back into full consciousness.

The four other patients—grouped in the same semicircle of folding chairs as Shelley and Anthony—were appropriately silent, giving Anthony space to find himself again. Alex was particularly pleased that Tom Lawson, the newest patient here, had read the mood of the room correctly and had held his tongue both during the exploration itself and in these first moments of aftermath. The group sessions could be startling for first-timers. Lawson had done well.

Slowly, Alex leaned slightly forward in his leather armchair, a tiny gesture but one sufficient to let the group know that he was ready to take them back into discussion. Each of them dutifully looked over to him. Except Tom Lawson, who was still staring with a puzzled fascination at Shelley.

"Perhaps somebody could fetch Anthony a glass of water?" Alex said. "Tom?"

Lawson turned to him. For a second, his eyes seemed as blank and confused as Esposito's, as if he too had recently been woken from deep recovery. "Oh," he said, coming back to the reality of the room. "Sure. No problem."

Alex—smiling in acknowledgment as Lawson stood and crossed to the water cooler to fill a paper cup—looked at Shelley.

She was leaning back in her chair now, doing some deep-breathing exercises. The exhaustion—physical as well as simply emotional—never seemed to lessen for her, Alex noted. Each time seemed as enervating as the one before. Though never worse. And her recovery time was always under a minute or two. He could safely assume this as a constant, he figured, if he were ever foolish enough to try to form equations within such an inexact science.

Lawson handed the cup of water to Anthony, who nodded his gratitude and took it. Alex watched as the seated man began to drink his water in his usual fashion; in tiny bird-like sips that allowed only a few drops of liquid at a time into his mouth. Lawson might have noticed this too, had he not shifted his attention almost immediately to Shelley.

"Do *you* need anything?" he asked her.

She gave Lawson a quick glance, shaking her head. "No," she said and, after a moment, "Thank you."

"Yes, thank you, Tom," Alex said. Not brusquely. Not at all. But business-like enough to send Lawson back to his seat, where his barely concealed double-take as he finally registered Esposito's idiosyncratic approach to drinking almost made Alex laugh out loud.

Moontown

"Well, Tom," he said. "We certainly threw you in at the deep end, didn't we?" He glanced briefly at the others, the subtle twinkle in his eyes giving them implicit permission to smile. "Quite a welcome to your first session." He shifted his gaze to Shelley and Anthony. "How are you guys doing?" he said.

Shelley didn't answer him immediately. Her concern was still with Esposito. "Are you okay, Anthony?" she asked him.

Esposito nodded. Even managed a small smile. "Yeah," he said. "Yeah. That was... intense."

Richie Nathanson, one of the other patients, an overweight and balding fifty-year-old, nodded in agreement. "No shit," he said. "You sounded *terrified*."

"What did you *see*?" Sarah Blackwood said. She was the pretty post-grad cellist who was in the study group more at her own request than because Alex thought it strictly necessary from a clinical point of view.

"What did *you* see, Shelley?" This from Margaret Paris, technically a colleague of Alex's—an associate professor over at the Humanities Department—but in this room simply another patient, and one who should know better than to try and direct the conversation.

Shelley locked eyes with Margaret, her expression vaguely troubled in a way that Alex didn't like but recognized, troubled the way it always was whenever she tried to explain (or even talk about) what she insisted on referring to as *this stuff*.

"I saw what Anthony saw," she said. "I was—"

Alex interrupted her.

"Hold on," he said. "Hold on. Let's help Tom get up to speed—and remind ourselves what we're doing here."

This was always the problem with his little band of phobics, their readiness to be interested in the details and specifics of their own and each other's terrors instead of maintaining focus on his preferred big picture. He paused until he was sure he had regained their attention.

"Fear is paralysis," he said. "Fear is a locked door, one that keeps us from the rest of the world. Fear is a monster that holds us trapped in the dark."

He knew that to some of the people here he was repeating himself, but repetition was, after all, a time-honored form of education. He held little brief with new-age notions of affirmation-as-reality, but if he could insert these thoughts and observations of his as mantra-like phrases in their heads, then he'd certainly be doing no harm and quite possibly be helping them.

"Our job here is to *confront* fear," he continued. "To see it clearly. To name it plainly. And when we do that…the door opens. When we do that, the light comes on. When we do that, the monster goes away."

He knew he'd ended on what could reductively be called an applause line, but he wasn't bothered at all by the collective silence that actually greeted his remarks. He recognized it as one of the good silences. His listeners were not confused, but attentive. Not doubtful, but hopeful. If not yet unafraid, then at least feeling the stirrings of the previously undreamed possibility of a life without fear.

Which is what made Shelley's naked discomfort with the rapt attention he had won from the others so bloody annoying. Look at her—looking at each of them in turn, her eyes troubled and brow furrowed as if the plain blossoming of hope in these people's faces was not something that should go unchallenged. Her tendency to second-guess and overthink was something he and she had talked about before, something that he'd tried to make clear was counterproductive in the context of the group-study, but was plainly something he needed to bring up again in their next one-on-one session.

"We're not really doing anything that standard therapeutic approaches in the outside world don't do," she said, her tone almost apologetic. "I think it's more about—"

Alex interrupted her, careful not to let any anger show in front of the others, careful that he at least not undercut the fragile faith that they were beginning to build in themselves.

"Now, now, Shelley," he said to her, his voice a careful imitation of gentle and affectionate mockery, "don't be so modest. Other therapeutic approaches don't have *you*."

He smiled warmly at her, holding her gaze just long enough to be sure she was quieted, and then looked out to take in the whole group again. Lawson, as the newcomer, was a useful anchor for what to the others would simply be more repetition, so Alex addressed his next remarks to him.

"Shelley's one of our brightest postgraduate students," he said. "But that alone doesn't begin to explain her importance here."

He let that dangle for a moment, allowing Lawson to feel and appreciate the mystery, before continuing.

"She's our secret weapon, Tom. Or, if you will, the secret operative we drop behind enemy lines. When our fears are buried so deep that we don't even know what they are, we need a guide through our own unconscious. Shelley's a natural empath, somebody who can go into the dark with us and help us find the beast."

Shelley was of course now casting her eyes down at her own lap, even though Margaret Paris was reaching over and patting her hand with proud affection and Esposito was nodding in grateful affirmation.

Lawson's reaction was odder.

He gazed at Shelley for an unembarrassed several seconds, his own face devoid of any readable expression, and then turned back to Alex.

Lawson smiled at him in a way that Alex didn't quite understand and didn't much like. As if Alex had just volunteered information not about Shelley, but about himself.

3

"Good God," said the man's voice, "you sure you're up to that?"

Shelley Campbell wondered to whom the question was addressed before realizing, with a sinking feeling, that it was apparently her.

She'd been standing at the counter of Johnnie's, the campus's retro-styled coffee shop, for only a couple of minutes and had just taken possession of a huge Black and White Malt, the prize with which she regularly rewarded herself after a group session. She felt she particularly deserved it today; Anthony's session had been both grueling and heart breaking. That was some dark shit his unconscious had been dragging around all these years, poor guy. Poor little boy, rather—she'd seen the child's reflection in the mirror just like he had, and knew that that was who the fear actually had its grip on, rather than the adult into whom he'd apparently grown up.

But it looked like she wasn't going to be allowed her reward without complication. There'd been no one else at the counter until a few seconds ago, when the guy who'd just spoken had ambled up. Her creep radar had tingled just a little when he arrived—because, come on, the counter was wide open, and he has to park himself less than two feet from her?—but she'd told herself not to overreact. Just a guy at a counter, probably jonesing more for a grilled cheese than a chick's phone number. But then he'd had to go and open his mouth.

She didn't look around. Not at first. Maybe he'd be cool, maybe just accept her silence—rationalize it as deafness rather than rejection, if he needed to—and let it go.

"I mean, that's a *lot* of shake," he said.

Or maybe not.

Swallowing her sigh, Shelley turned to look at him. He was four or five years older than her. Kind of handsome actually, but—handsome or not—her tolerance for intrusive strangers was not high, and she was about to tell this one to piss off and quit bothering her when she recognized him.

The new guy from group.

Took her a second to search for his name, but she got it.

"Tom," she said.

"Right," he said, and smiled. Smiled in a way that was both amused and forgiving. Like she'd just had some weird little Alzheimer's preview, because of *course* she knew his name. Like they were friends. Which didn't, like, creep her out or anything, but still…

Waving to the counterman to get his attention, Tom—*Lomax? Laughlin?* Lawson, *that was it*—gestured at the shake in front of Shelley on the counter. "Could I get one of those?" he said.

The counterman nodded and turned to the chrome and somewhat overstylized fountain to prepare the order, and Tom swung back to face Shelley. "I'm sorry," he said. "I'm being presumptuous. Do you mind if I join you?"

She hesitated. It was one of those awkward moments—you know, where you *do* mind if someone joins you but you don't have a dead grandmother or a homework-eating dog handy—but what was she going to do? So she smiled—graciously, she hoped—and said okay and followed Tom across the floor to the vacant booth that he'd indicated with a *shall we?* nod of his head.

The counterman was only moments behind them and, once he'd delivered the shake and left, Tom looked down at it with an expression that was half amused and half alarmed.

"Wow," he said. "A Black and White Malt. Very fifties. I feel like I should be wearing a letterman sweater."

Shelley looked at him. "Interesting that you'd want to be the dumb jock instead of Danny Zuko," she said.

"Oh, I know my place," Tom said. "And, apparently, you know your movies."

Knew her movies? Jesus. She supposed he was trying for a light compliment, but it was *Grease*, for fuck's sake, not some subtitled art-house rarity. She spared him that thought, though, and gave a little half-hearted smile instead.

"Anyway," he said, "can I ask you something?"

"Sure."

"Well, apart from the requisite type-A personality—which he seems to have in spades even if he dresses it up in postseventies nonconfrontational drag—how come *Drayton* runs those sessions? It seems like *you* have the—"

Shelley interrupted him.

"No," she said. "You don't understand. The whole study's part of my Ph.D. thesis, but I'm not a doctor. Not yet. So Alex—Doctor Drayton—has to supervise any actual clinical work."

"But it's your brain child?" Tom said.

"Pretty much, I suppose."

She wanted to leave it there, far from ready to start volunteering information to this guy—particularly after that throwaway and snide little character-sketch of Alex—but he just sat there, open-eyed and smiling, eager to hear more and letting her own silence make her uncomfortable enough to give it to him.

"But bringing in real patients—you know, real people with real problems—that was his idea. It's just that I have, you know..." She mimed quote marks in the air. *"The gift."*

Oh, and there it was, ladies and gentlemen—that stupid self-mocking tone to which she always retreated when forced to speak of the special thing she could do. She was ashamed of her shame. Contemptuous of the contempt she pretended to feel for her talent. But apparently incapable of separating her respect for the thing itself from what she feared might look like self-aggrandizement.

If Tom saw any of that confusion of feeling, he certainly didn't acknowledge it. He was still just sitting there. Ready for facts, and fuck the subtext. More Joe Friday than Sigmund Freud.

"And Alex thinks I can really help people," she said. "I don't know. I..."

Her voice trailed off, and she watched him register—finally—the obvious fact that she wasn't yet completely at ease with her role in the group sessions.

"Well," he said, "you certainly seemed to help... what's his name?"

"Anthony," Shelley said.

"Anthony. Esposito, right?" He waited for a confirming nod from her before continuing. "How much of, you know, what you saw did you know was coming?"

"None," Shelley said. "None of it. And neither did Anthony. That's the point."

Tom nodded. "Recovery of buried memories," he said. It

wasn't a question.

"Right," said Shelley. "The problem that brings someone to therapy might bear no apparent relation to what the actual root problem is. Anthony came to Alex originally because of a specific OCD—you know what that is, right? Obsessive-compulsive disorder?—it took him about ninety minutes to eat a candy bar. Steak dinner could be a day's work."

"Okay," said Tom, drawing out the first syllable in order to change the word into that prickish shorthand code for *that's really fucking weird*.

Shelley was annoyed but pretended not to notice. "He'd slice and dice his food—any food—into pieces anybody else would regard as...well, as *crumbs*...and then eat them. One at a time. Slowly."

Tom kept looking at her for a moment and then got it. "He was afraid of choking," he said.

"Had been for most of his life," said Shelley. "Every phobia we have is rooted in something, but Alex couldn't get through to whatever the trigger was for Anthony. The only other...anomaly...in his life was that he'd suffered from terrible nightmares since he was a kid. He'd wake up sweating and screaming but could never remember the dreams themselves. Alex figured that's where the secret was, so..."

"So he sent you in," Tom said, with a smile that Shelley figured was supposed to be supportive but had a little more well-aren't-*you*-special spin on it than he was perhaps aware of.

"He puts both of us in a mild hypnotic state," she said, "and then I...take us through. And we locate the repressed memory—either a real incident or, as in Anthony's case, a dream."

"And you really *see* it?" Tom said, with an eager interest that seemed to be the first honestly unguarded question he had asked. "I mean, I know you both described it to us afterward, but you really..."

Shelley broke in. "Like I'm right there with them," she said. "Not seeing through their eyes but really *there*. In the memory-space." She paused for a moment, derailed from explaining the theory by her memory of Anthony's memory. "That poor little boy must've been so scared," she said. "So scared that his conscious mind wouldn't even let him remember it. But his unconscious stayed on guard for the rest of his life. Trying to protect him from the Ragman."

"And that's all it was?" Tom said, and then caught himself. "Sorry, I don't mean that the way it sounds. I mean, it *was* just a dream? There never was a Ragman?"

"Not really. There'd been a guy—it was all over the news thirty years ago—he'd kidnapped a child and hidden her in an abandoned factory. He'd shoved a gag in her mouth and left her there. Before he got back, the little girl suffocated."

"Oh, man."

"Adults probably kept the details from other kids, like Anthony. Well-meaning, you know? He was only seven. But it's never a good idea to keep secrets from children. They hear whispers, rumors, phrases..."

Tom completed the thought for her. "And make constructs of their own to explain what the grown-ups won't tell them."

Shelley nodded. "Anthony's imagination filled in the gaps in that kidnapping story, made it much worse than it was."

"Mmm," Tom said, and nodded. Chewed on the thought for a second or two and then looked off to the side, as if searching for something. Turned out to be a memory.

Moontown

"When I was six years old," he said, "a neighbor—old guy across the street, Mister Brown, never knew his first name, still don't—he killed himself. Like you said, the adults tried to keep it from the kids, the details at least. But I overheard my mom and another neighbor talking. Wasn't paying much attention, busy turning Optimus Prime back into a truck, but then a phrase leapt out at me. Weird, I can't even remember whether it was my mom's voice or the neighbor lady's, but I remember the phrase, alright. *He put his head in the oven.* Now, I know *now* what that means—the guy gassed himself, right?"

He paused for a moment, looking at Shelley as if, oddly, the question wasn't rhetorical, as if he still actually needed the reassurance of agreement on that point.

"Right," she said. "Gassed himself."

"Right. But I didn't know that then. I didn't know you could run the gas without the flame." He looked at her again. "You see where I'm going with this?"

Unfortunately, she did. Tom nodded as he saw her complete the picture in her head.

"Yep," he said. "That's right. For years I figured this guy had somehow had the will, the strength even, to keep his head in a *lit* oven until it burned to a cinder. That was the image I got. A cooked, blackened thing, like some rib roast left unattended till it was practically coal. Couldn't get that picture out of my head for *years*. Still can't, actually. Even though I know that isn't what happened."

"Well, thanks so much for putting it in mine," Shelley said, and then paused, suddenly wondering if what he'd just told her had been more than some marginally grotesque attempt at sharing. "Oh," she said. "Is that... I mean, does that relate to whatever it is that brought you to—"

"You mean why I joined the study group?"

"Yeah."

"Not as far as I know." He looked at her for a moment. "I'm a klepto."

"Oh." That was articulate, Shelley. Well done.

"Yeah." He nodded, a little abashedly.

"You…"

"Steal things."

"Right."

"Right. Better hang on to your purse, there."

Infuriatingly, she actually felt her hand wanting to inch its way over to where her purse lay on the table between them. She managed not to do it, but wasn't sure she'd managed to keep the desire to do so from showing on her face.

"Just kidding," Tom said. "Seriously, I've got it under control. I mean, you know, for the most part."

"Started when you were a kid?" she said.

"Doesn't everything?"

Shelley heard that. She gave him a wry smile, a genuine one, and stood up. She was surprised by how much of her Black and White she'd managed to drink while they'd been talking. "Listen," she said, "I gotta go. Nothing to do with what you just said, honestly. I just got somewhere to be."

She put her hand out across the table and Tom half-rose to shake it. He seemed surprised that she was leaving so abruptly.

"Oh. Okay," he said. "Sure. Well, listen, this was…"

Shelley knew why his voice had trailed off. He didn't have the next word. Not an appropriate one, anyway. *This was…* what? Nice? Fun? She enjoyed his discomfort for a second, but was about to step in to let him off the hook, when he tried another tack.

"Shelley," he said. "That's short for...?"

"Michelle," Shelley said. "Michelle Campbell. Not really *short for*, I guess. I mean, two syllables each." Good God, who'd hit her babble switch while she wasn't looking?

Tom smiled. "Tom Lawson," he said. Kind of formally. Like some mutual acquaintance had just put them together. Shelley realized he was still holding her hand.

"It was nice to meet you, Tom," she said, and took her hand back.

"Not a doctor, huh?" he said. "So we wouldn't be breaking any doctor-patient etiquette if we—"

Whoa. Throttle back, Sparky. He was obviously about to ask for a date. She cut him off quickly.

"I don't think that's a good idea," she said, not unkindly. "I'm sorry."

Tom nodded a taking-it-like-a-man nod. A pretty good one, really. Eye contact didn't waver. Smile didn't falter. "Same group, and all," he said in an understanding tone.

"Right."

"Rain check for when I'm a fully functioning member of society?"

"Maybe," she said. She didn't mean it, but what the hell you gonna do? She gave him as warm a smile as she could manage and headed for the door.

*

Tom, still standing, picked up his ridiculous drink and sucked a mouthful of its sugary overkill through its infantile straw. His eyes never left Shelley's pert little denim-clad ass until she was out the door.

Peter Atkins

The coffee shop's large plate-glass window allowed him to keep her in sight until she was lost in the crowd of undergrads weaving across the quad.

He sat down in the booth again, pushing his glass away from him across the table. From an inside pocket, he pulled out his BlackBerry and selected his virtual notebook.

Fingers jabbing rapidly, he wrote down three names in list form: *Alex Drayton; Anthony Esposito; Michelle Campbell.*

4

Thank God for the shuffle function.

Shelley couldn't understand people who took their morning or evening runs to preselected playlists. What boost were you going to get from songs you *knew* were coming? How was that going to help you pick up the pace? How was that going to lift your heart with the thrill of an unexpected favorite when your lungs were starting to ache or your legs were threatening to quit?

Like right now, for example. If she hadn't just experienced that last beautifully random segue from Lily Allen to Arthur Alexander, she doubted she'd have sailed past her apartment building's door, ready to put in one more circuit of her usual three-block stretch even though the sun was already setting behind the Silverlake hills.

The neighborhood was safe—*well, safe enough,* added the cautionary voice of Second-Guess Shell—but she wasn't an idiot and she didn't like to jog in the dark. And night fell very fast in Los Angeles.

Still, the circuit took her less than five minutes on average so one more song and she'd be back at her building. Maybe two more if Arthur Alexander was to be followed by something short and furious, something old-school punk *(thank you Jamie Gilroy, November 2002 to February 2003).* Or maybe not even half of one song if, please God no, what showed up next was one of her few keep-forgetting-to-fucking-delete examples of prog-rock *(thanks a bunch Dennis Duchser, two foolish weeks in July '05).*

Her friend Molly was infuriatingly dismissive of Shelley's devotion to the party-shuffle. "Girl, you're just playing the *radio*," she'd say. "One song following another, that's all it is. But you're all up in yourself, like you're inventing something."

"But it's Radio Shelley," Shelley would explain. "The greatest radio station in the world. Where you never know what's coming next, but you know you're going to like it."

Case in point; here came something now. Not punk. Not prog. Here came a fabulous guilty pleasure, the lunatic and illegal mash-up of *Waiting for the Man* and *Sugar, Sugar* synthesized a couple of years ago by some bedroom genius with time on his hands and Acid software on his laptop. Just great. Just fucking great. Better than either of the originals, ISHO —the Velvets' gravitas cutting Jeff Barry's glucose, which in turn sweetened Lou Reed's dyspepsia. Accompanied by Shelley's steady energized breathing, it carried her safely home through the gathering dark.

*

Showered and relaxed, one towel wrapped around her body and another turbaned over her hair, Shelley walked into her kitchen, her left hand flicking almost unconsciously at some stray water droplets on her right shoulder.

She crossed to her fridge, opened it, took out a quart-size apple juice, and had a good hefty swig directly from the carton.

As she was swallowing, she noticed that the kitchen blind was still open. This side of her building faced directly over the street to the banked hills on the other side, hills that were too steep for even the most ludicrously ambitious of LA developers to try to perch houses on. There was one theoretical lamppost halfway up the nearest slope as a gestural claim that civilization didn't stop at that side of the road but it was out more often than it was on, and tonight was no exception. The hills were nothing but black shapes now, darker than the night sky above them, which was illuminated into an astonishing midnight blue by the large and almost-full moon that hovered not too far above the hills' false horizon.

Shelley stared at the moon for a moment—very *present* tonight, she couldn't help thinking, its Rorschach features particularly persuasive, almost insistent—then pulled her blind closed.

She replaced the carton and closed the fridge door. The accidental collage of magnets, homilies, snapshots, and clipped newspaper cartoons that covered it—usually and inevitably rendered invisible by the familiarity of their everyday presence—suddenly struck her as if with the shock of the new, as if they were demanding her attention, as if suddenly they were as insistent as the moon, or as if the moon itself had, in that single magical instant of her undefended regard, trained her eye to see through the gauze of the familiar and to focus on the usually unremembered.

And of course it was Jen on whom her eye finally, ineluctably, settled.

It was just a stupid Polaroid—colors already fading, taken on a flirtatious whim by some guy they hardly knew at a frat party they'd soon forgotten—but it was the best picture she had of her lost friend. Not best as in there were plenty of better ones but this was all she had, but best as in best. Jen looked so beautiful. So young. So vivacious. So happy. So fucking *alive*.

PETER ATKINS

She was three years younger in the picture than Shelley was now, three years younger than she herself would have been, and she was smiling at the unseen photographer—a big smile, one just on the edge of open-hearted laughter—both delightedly flattered by his attention and charmingly dismissive of any romantic ambitions he may have been harboring.

Shelley stared at the picture, caught by it in a way she hadn't been for months, feeling the stirrings of sense-memory of the moment it had been taken, almost hearing Eminem screaming at people to lose themselves in the music the moment, almost smelling the ghostly traces of cigarettes and Chanel, almost feeling, beneath Jen's soft and delicate skin, her dear and precious heartbeat.

Hardly aware she was doing it, she reached out her hand to let the tip of her finger touch the captured face…

*

The hospital morgue wasn't quite the washed-out white and chrome space that television and movies led you to believe—the lighting was softer and more diffuse and there were humanizing touches here and there as if the staff knew that for some visitors this was as close to a funeral chapel as their loved ones were going to get—but it was every bit as cold as you'd expect it to be.

And the people stored there were every bit as dead.

Jen, pale and lifeless, was lying on a cold metal slab, her soul irretrievably absent and her flesh utterly empty. Beneath the minimal mercy of the white cotton sheet would be the red scars and the black stitching, the yellow bruises and the purple lividity, but above the hem of the sheet only her naked head and shoulders were visible and they were singularly unmarked.

Moontown

Which you'd think would have been a blessing.

But it wasn't. Because somehow the sight of wounds would have helped. Somehow the presence of visible damage, the unavoidable evidence of undeniable physical devastation, would have helped make more sense of this... what?... of this evacuated *flesh, of this dead meat and the spiritual void within it.*

Back in the real moment of Shelley's viewing of the corpse of her friend, the only sounds had been the hum of refrigeration and the hissing of other machines. But this flash-memory was crueler and less clinical in its choice of soundtrack. Like an audio-visual mash-up from YouTube in Hell, *the morgue was filled by dreadful noise—a jarring, cacophonous medley of tortured metal screeching as if in pain and human voices screaming in terror. And almost buried in the hideous sonic cocktail— but horribly, poignantly, clear enough—Jen's beautiful lost voice whooping in incongruous joy:*

"Gonna have some fun tonight!"

*

Shelley jerked her hand back from the Polaroid as if stung.

She exhaled, shaking in horror, and closed her eyes against the old memory and the still-fresh pain.

5

Taylor Smith was at the window again.

He had his back to the other seven-year-olds, all of whom were already busy with the morning's assigned activities, and was staring out of the group study annex at the campus quad.

Shelley was giving him a moment, choosing to believe that all Taylor was seeing through the window was what anybody else would see—the crisp sunlight and clear air of a Los Angeles October and the scores of regular undergrads and coeds crisscrossing the quad on their way to or from classes. She couldn't see Taylor's face, but she knew what his expression would be. It'd be what it always was in his silent spells: impassive; almost solemn; distressingly mature.

On paper, and according to his previous doctors, the pediatric psychologists with whom Alex Drayton had conferred before accepting him into the program, Taylor was no more troubled than the other children who had been approved for observation and care as part of Shelley's group-study project. But Shelley thought there was a level to Taylor's issues that nobody had yet been able to access and that Taylor himself was not willing, or perhaps not even able, to talk about. It was that look that came over his face that niggled at her. She knew she was seeing something in it that nobody else did and she knew that—*hoped* that—she might be wrong. It was a calm expression, was the consensus, a look that said that Taylor was finding a quiet place within himself, a place away from his troubles, rather than a part of them. But Shelley didn't read the calmness as coming from a secret place of sanctuary or peace. Instead, she found herself thinking, appallingly, of the wiped-clean quietude that combat-zone photographers found on the faces of the shell-shocked. Shelley wondered, whenever Taylor stared out at the world with that particular expression on his face, just what it was that he was actually seeing.

The nine other kids, all within a year or two of Taylor's age and all with somewhat similar behavioral issues, were definitely doing better on the play-well-with-others front than he was.

Molly and Shelley had done their best to make the annex room that they had been given for this branch of the group-study project look like a regular classroom, open-plan and kid-friendly. The center of the room was full of cushions, mats, construction toys, and the like, all as brightly colored and as inviting as possible, and the other kids were right now engaged in the collaborative building of a large plastic playhouse from various simple and prefabricated pieces.

Shelley found herself once again thanking God for Molly Edwards, knowing that she herself would frankly have had no idea how to create an environment for the kids that felt unthreatening and familiar. It was that very aspect, though, that seemed to be second nature for Molly. Technically, she was here as a county-appointed child psychologist to supervise whatever work Shelley managed to do with the children, but she'd effortlessly—and without ever announcing it as a strategy—found the cover roles for the two of them that seemed most natural and nonalarming to the kids. If asked who precisely were these women with whom they spent two mornings a week, Shelley knew that each of the children, without needing time to think about it, would have answered that Ms. Edwards was a teacher and that Ms. Campbell was a teacher's assistant.

Again, they'd not *told* the children this, but simply let them feel it out, let them make sense of it for themselves. Shelley would have liked to have believed that their collective instinct to cast Molly in the senior role was due entirely to Molly being old enough to be *her* mother, let alone theirs, but she knew that chronological age had very little to do with it. It was way more atavistic than that. Kids apparently knew on a cellular level that there were those to whom you could give shit and that there were those to whom you couldn't. And Molly Edwards had never taken shit in her life. Shelley, on the other hand, despite *looking* like an adult, despite having in fact a couple inches of height on Molly, was perceived not as a grownup but as a playmate, not as a den-mother but as just one of the pack, some overgrown cub with pretensions and a paycheck. They *liked* her enough, thank Christ, but if she wanted them to do something that they didn't feel immediately like doing then she'd have to persuade them or, worse, bargain with them. Whereas Molly could tell them to juggle broken glass and they'd be bleeding from major arteries before thinking to ask why.

Shelley stepped the few feet from where the playhouse construction was underway to Molly's desk. "Taylor's still looking out the window," she said quietly.

"Well, tell him to stop," said Miss Pragmatist 1982, without looking up from the paperwork she was assiduously filing in what she called her fuck-it-till-they-write-a-second-time drawer.

"Taylor?" Shelley called across the room to the boy.

Moontown

"Don't you want to join in?"

Her voice was gentle, which was fine, and tentative, which wasn't, and she didn't have to look back at Molly to feel the smirk on her friend's face.

"Ooh, check you out," Molly said in mock-admiration. "Getting all *Ilsa, She-Wolf of the SS* on his ass."

Much to Shelley's relief, however, the seven-year-old turned from the window and looked across the room at her. He was blinking a little, as if bringing her back into focus, but the frozen impassivity was gone from his face.

Shelley smiled encouragingly at him and, after a second or two, Taylor tried for a smile in return. It was a little gestural, a little monkey-see-monkey-do, as if Taylor had just landed his rocket on an alien planet and was doing his best to imitate the facial tics of the natives, but—even though it suggested, as heartbreakingly as ever, that smiling wasn't something Taylor was particularly used to—at least it was there.

Shelley nodded at the junior construction crew who were already more than half-finished with the building of the playhouse. "You want to give your friends a hand?" she said to Taylor, and was pleased to hear a little more steel in her voice.

Taylor didn't answer her directly but he did start walking across the room towards the other children.

Shelley's initial burst of pleasure at this modicum of progress was tempered almost immediately by disappointment as Taylor stopped several feet shy of the in-progress playhouse and, rather than begin to interact with his classmates, instead began to circle the bright yellow plastic walls and bright red plastic roof of the incomplete structure somewhat warily, reserving the most suspicious of his glances for what would soon be the interior.

Molly had come out from behind her desk now and was standing beside Shelley. Both of them watched Taylor's investigative and guarded circling, each of them trying not to be too obvious about it.

"It's alright," Molly said privately to Shelley—she had this wonderful knack of speaking at what appeared to be the volume of a normal adult conversation without ever attracting the attention of the kids. "Let's not push."

"No, of course not," Shelley said. Unlike Molly, she had to almost whisper whenever they were this near the kids and she didn't want them to hear her. "I just wish he'd..." She left the thought unfinished, not out of reticence but because she realized she didn't know what it was she'd been intending to say.

Molly knew, though. "What?" she said, gently. "That he'd turn into a normal kid?" She was right, of course. That was always the wish.

Shelley turned to face Molly—Taylor was continuing to circle the playhouse but didn't seem about to do anything else, and the other kids didn't seem bothered by him—and gave a wry smile. "With one wave of my magic wand," she said.

"Nothing wrong with that," said Molly. "It's a sweet wish."

"Yeah," Shelley said. "No wand, though."

"Not one you can see, anyway," Molly said. "But a big heart, Shelley. And in the long run that's more important."

A sudden multi-voiced burst of childish laughter drew their eyes instantly back to the center of the room.

The laughter turned out to have nothing to do with Taylor —who was apparently done with his wary reconnaissance of the playhouse and was heading over to the netted area in the corner of the room where several oversized balls were stashed—but was centered around Cameron Weintraub, another seven-year-old boy for whom the construction of the playhouse had apparently grown tiresome. Cameron had unilaterally elected to take the classroom activities in another direction and brighten his fellow kids' morning by lowering his pants and showing them his ass.

Cameron, Shelley had to acknowledge, had the kind of instinct for popular entertainment that most television executives would kill for, because the butt display was a huge hit. Every other kid had stopped working on the playhouse to stare at him—calmly bent over in an inverted V, head resting peacefully on the floor and a beatific smile on his face—and to greet his efforts with delightedly enthusiastic laughter.

"Fuck me," said Molly, fortunately still in her magically-inaudible-to-kids voice. "Already? I haven't even had my frigging coffee yet."

Despite her words, Shelley noticed Molly had difficulty keeping a grin off her own face as she started across to the kids, leaving Shelley behind and calling out to Cameron.

"Cameron!" she shouted. "You know that I think it's the cutest tush in the world, but what have we said about keeping some things private?"

The others were still laughing as Molly reached the boy and yanked his pants back up.

Shelley, looking over at them and fighting her own instinct to join in the laughter, suddenly sensed that she was being stared at.

She looked over to the far side of the almost-finished playhouse, forgotten now by everybody else in the room, to see that Taylor was gazing directly at her with a quizzical, almost appraising, look on his face. His arms were stretched up above his head and, between them, he was holding a large white plastic ball, almost two feet in diameter.

That flat lost expression was back on his face now and, as Shelley watched him, he angled the ball out and forward, so that it hovered overhead of the playhouse's half-completed red plastic roof.

"Taylor...?" Shelley said, her voice quiet and unsure.

Taylor, keeping his unreadable eyes fixed unerringly on Shelley, made no response at all. Other than to suddenly fling the white ball downwards with a strength and a quiet, contained fury that was all the more disturbing for the unchanging blankness of his face.

The ball smashed through the roof of the playhouse, which collapsed in on itself instantly.

One of the little girls screamed.

6

He felt extremely grateful to whichever long-dead city planner had decided back in the nineteen-thirties that the trees on this particular stretch of sidewalk wouldn't be the ubiquitous Southern California palms.

Very hard to hide behind a palm.

These cypresses, though, with their dense, tightly packed foliage that not only grew usefully wide enough to conceal someone but also grew very low on the trunk, leaving only a couple of feet bare at the bottom, were practically custom-made for a person to stand unobtrusively behind and to observe whatever it was that a person might want to observe.

It was hardly ideal, of course. The perfect point for observation is a point where the observer is not himself able to be observed. And, despite the shelter of the cypress and the gathering darkness of the coming night, he was hardly invisible. He was still on a sidewalk, after all. There were still single-story houses and two-story four-plexes behind him. There were still cars being parked for the evening by people making their way to those houses or apartments. People who might wonder what exactly he was doing standing behind a tree and looking at the apartment building on the opposite side of the road.

But people were surprisingly good at minding their own business for the most part. And it wasn't like he was an idiot, advertising what he was doing. It wasn't like he was pressed up against the tree, pulling its branches surreptitiously apart to peer through them. He was just a guy standing on the sidewalk. A little close to that tree, maybe, but just a guy standing on the sidewalk. Probably waiting for his ride. And he looked presentable enough, he was sure. Hardly a low-life. Hardly threatening. And he wasn't going to be here very long.

Unless her routine had changed.

It was, in fact, already a little later than he expected it would be. Late enough that the near-full moon had risen already and was climbing above the hills on the far side of her building. It wasn't the smartest thing to jog in the dark. What was she thinking? He hoped nothing unpleasant had happened to her.

From somewhere far back in the city, a siren sounded piercingly above the ceaseless hum of general traffic—just a brief warning burst, as if some idiot civilian car was being told to give way—and, from deep in the hills beyond the building, a single confused coyote responded to the call, its howl eerily and perfectly matching the pitch of the siren's ugly and jagged note.

His eyes flicked over for a moment to what seemed to be the direction of the animal's cry, and when he looked back she was there. Funny how that happens. A watched pot never boils.

Shelley was turning the final corner at the far end of her block. Perfectly safe. Hardly late at all, really. And the brown paper bag she was clutching in her left hand explained the couple of minutes' discrepancy. She must have run in somewhere—maybe the convenience store on Micheltorena? —and picked something up. Nice domestic detail. Little variant in the routine, but hardly relevant.

Christ, she was *really* in shape, he thought. A not entirely dispassionate observation, but what could she expect? Tiny white tank-top, tight black running shorts. Come on.

He tightened his position behind the tree a little to make sure she couldn't see him unless she really had reason to look. Turning slowly and carefully to keep her in sight through the semi-obscuring filter of the cypress branches, he watched as she trotted along the block to her building's front door, slowing the pace of the final fifty yards for a brief cool-down period. Very wise. Helps avoid cramping.

She closed the front door behind her, and he looked up to the second floor, waiting to see the light come on in her living room.

*

Almost as if she'd triggered it, the phone started ringing as soon as Shelley clicked on the living room light. She was tempted to let the machine take it but decided to pick it up instead.

Took about ten seconds to make her wish she hadn't.

The call—the part of it she heard, in any case—was simple and informative.

There might have been more. There might have been expressions of regret or sympathy. There might have been more details, or speculations as to reason or cause.

But if there were, Shelley didn't hear them. The phone had already fallen from her fingers by then and the voice at the other end was babbling inaudibly from somewhere near her feet as she simply stood and stared, the sweat from her evening's run suddenly freezing on her horrified skin.

*

Peter Atkins

The nicer parts of Cheviot Hills were glimpses from a dream of a suburban America where post-war prosperity and opportunity never went away. The streets, generously wide and impeccably paved, rose and fell gently and slowly. The lawns were manicured and the fences well kept. The splendid houses were quietly beautiful, without a trace of ostentation or swagger.

But there were three cop cars at the corner of Mason and Kingswell, and there would soon be yellow crime-scene tape drawn across the front door of 3462 Mason.

Inside the house, past the crowd of hard-working professionals—uniformed cops, detectives, photographers and paramedics—was the crime scene itself.

It was a small room set behind a much larger lounge, the kind of small room that used to be called a den or a hobby room.

It was dominated by several display cases, some tall and shelved, some low and deep with slanted glass covers. Each of the cases was filled with innumerable and carefully mounted vintage matchbook covers, all of them from nightclubs, hotels, and restaurants of the nineteen-thirties and -forties, their art-deco graphics redolent of a lost age of urban sophistication.

Between two of the cases, the homeowner was in what a neighbor had confirmed to one of the policemen was his favorite leather armchair, the place where he came to enjoy his collection.

Anthony Esposito's legs were crossed at the ankles. His palms were resting on the arms of the chair. His head was tilted back on the gentle curve of the leather, and his dead eyes were wide open in frozen terror.

Moontown

Anthony's cheeks were distended, and his mouth wide open.

It was stuffed with multicolored rags and tatters, some of them dangling like rats' tails over his lower lip.

7

"I think it was suicide," Alex said.

He waited for Shelley to overreact.

"Are you kidding me?" she said. Almost shouted, in fact. She half sat up in the recliner, trying to turn to look at him.

He was in his usual chair behind the big La-Z-Boy recliner because he'd suggested—knowing how distraught Shelley would naturally be over Anthony's death—that they have their conversation about it as one of their private sessions. He'd been pleased with how readily she'd acquiesced to the suggestion, how she'd accepted the idea that it might be better to talk to him as her therapist than as her colleague, but he'd also expected moments of resistance like this one. Rather than tell her to lie back down, he simply kept his voice calm and reasonable so that it would be her choice.

"No, Shelley," he said, "I'm not kidding. And I believe you know me well enough to trust that I wouldn't kid about something as sad and as serious as this."

She settled. A little, at least. His voice helped, he knew, as did the drawn translucent blinds that tamed the morning sun into a dimmer and more intimate light.

"Suicide?" she said. Still with a tone of disbelief. But quieter at least, and closer to an honest question than a rebuttal.

"Well," he said, "I think you should know that the police are leaning that way, too. There was, after all, no forced entry, no sign of struggle. Nothing was stolen or damaged. Their only hesitation, I think, is that—to them, at least—it's all so... odd."

"Odd?!"

"Shelley, please," he said. "Breathe. Relax."

She lay back more fully, which was good. But her voice took on a petulant tone. "Don't treat me as if I'm being irrational, Alex," she said. "I'm upset for a reason!" And then she added, as if she actually thought he might need it explaining: "Anthony's dead!"

"Yes, he is," Alex said. "And that's an undeniable tragedy." He let her hear that for a moment, let her take in the fact that she wasn't the only one to feel the depth of this situation. "But it is not your fault, Shelley. It's very important that you acknowledge that. Anthony was an extremely troubled man."

"Troubled enough to choke himself to death?" she said. "Jesus, can you even *do* that? Will your body even *let* you?"

"Technically, he died of fright, not suffocation."

"You're saying he scared himself to death?" she said. "Never mind the how—*why* would he do that?"

She was plainly finding it difficult to move beyond argument, Alex saw, and decided that perhaps engaging her would actually get her through this more quickly. "And what are *you* saying?" he said, allowing a little confrontation into his voice. And then just a smidgeon of ridicule: "That the *Ragman* did it? That Anthony was killed by a creature from his childhood imagination?"

Well, that shut her up for a moment. He saw her staring out into the room. It was unfair to expect her to answer it, of course. It did, after all, sound more than a little ridiculous once he'd said it aloud for her. He decided to press the point.

"That can't really be what you're thinking, can it?" he said.

"That the Ragman was *real* and that…what…that he waited all these years till Anthony *remembered* him? Presumably in order to enhance his enjoyment of killing him?"

Shelley made a noise of dismissal, as if of course that wasn't what she'd been thinking. "You honestly think Anthony shoved those rags in his own mouth?" she said.

Alex let her question hang there for a moment, let her use the silence to answer it for herself. "It's clear that we let something loose in him the other day," Alex said. "A memory that certainly *needed* to be loosened. But…"

He paused again, to let her hear him sigh, let her hear that he was steeling himself to go somewhere unpleasant.

"…but I fear there's a possibility that Anthony may have embraced that memory in a way other than we might have expected or wanted."

"Embraced it in *what* way?" Shelley said. "What do you mean?"

"May I make an observation?" he said, shifting his tone back now to the calm and the clinical. "Although his dreams began some years earlier, they were a constant companion to Anthony as he went through the rigors of puberty, which is —I think we can agree here—an age both of profound imprinting and of profound confusion. Yes?"

"Yes."

"Yes. Many kinds of confusion. Directional. Emotional." He took a beat there. Just a small one. Just enough. "Sexual."

He sensed, rather than saw, Shelley's body stiffen as if she were suddenly on guard. "What?" she said.

"I take it you've heard of autoerotic asphyxiation?"

Shelley was silent for a second or so. He regretted that he couldn't see her face. When she finally spoke, he could hear the effort she was making to keep her tone free of judgment. But the subtext of embarrassed disgust survived her best intentions. "You mean those people who half-hang themselves and... and jerk off?" she said.

"It's supposed to prolong the orgasm," he said.

"But Anthony wasn't... I mean, he was fully clothed. There was no evidence that he..."

"No," he said. "No evidence, you're right. Perhaps his intentions were still unformed or unconscious. Perhaps matters didn't get as far as they might have. But what I'm saying is this: in some sad and confused part of his mind, Anthony may have folded his anxiety into his erotica. If he did, he'd be far from alone in doing so. Sometimes what terrifies us, excites us too. It's a fact, perhaps a disturbing one, that fear can sometimes produce the same physical results as arousal."

"You mean sexual arousal," Shelley said, as if she just wanted to keep things clear. He was charmed by her tone's quite convincing imitation of detached clinical interest.

"Indeed," he said. "Hanged men die with erections, Shelley. Ejaculation isn't unknown. And women get wet when they're frightened. It's an atavistic response, the animal body sidestepping the mind and suggesting surrender—sexual surrender—as an escape strategy in the face of danger."

He knew that he'd let his voice become a little lower and more intimate than was perhaps entirely wise, but trusted that she was concentrating more on what he was saying than on how he was saying it. He leaned forward in his chair, just a little, not enough to make her feel he was invading her space, but enough to let him see more clearly over her shoulder and to allow him to look properly at her legs, stretched out on the recliner and crossed primly at the ankles. She was wearing jeans today, as was usual for their sessions. Sometimes, though, she wore a skirt, which he always enjoyed. He'd not so far been able to work out what it was that prompted her decision on those things, whether there was an element of reward involved.

He realized that she hadn't yet responded to his last comment, was simply lying there as if waiting passively to see what he would say, or do, next.

He allowed himself one more moment to breathe in the rich scent of possibility, and then chose to let it go. He leaned back in his seat again and made his voice brisk and business-like, as if he were in a lecture room rather than their small and private space.

"My point is this," he said. "Anthony may have embraced his fear in entirely the wrong way. I don't think that it was his intention to die. He was… flirting, if you will, rather than seeking actual consummation. But he went too far. The fear wasn't in a flirtatious mood. It took him. By force. And stopped his heart."

Shelley's voice was tentative. She was wanting to believe him, he could tell, but still very troubled. "Even if that's true," she said, "I still helped it happen. It's still…" She couldn't say it.

"Your fault?" Alex said.

"Yes," she said, and her voice was tiny and sad.

"No," he said. "That simply isn't true."

She wasn't convinced. "We should have gone more slowly," she said. "We should have followed up. Should have paid more attention to the possible consequences of what we were doing."

"Perhaps so," Alex acknowledged. "We should certainly

take more care the next time."

Shelley suddenly sat bolt upright and swung around to face him, putting her feet on the floor. He wasn't entirely surprised, though he naturally preferred that he be the one to signify the end of a session. He allowed a little of that disappointment to show on his face as he straightened up further in his chair, but Shelley seemed to be too shocked at what he'd just said to notice.

"Next time?" she said. "Now you've got to be kidding. There isn't going to be a next time. We need to stop, consider, rethink our whole approach."

Alex furrowed his brow at her. "Why would I be kidding? I'm not kidding at all," he said. "These are people who need our help, Shelley. What are you suggesting? That we simply abandon them at this point? Just as we've begun to give them hope?"

Shelley shook her head at him. "I think we have very different opinions about how they'd all feel, given what just happened."

"But what signal do you think we'd be sending to them if we were to cancel the sessions?" he said.

"That we're not... *reckless*. That we care about them as people, not just about the study itself."

"No," he said. "They'd think we were afraid. Worse, they'd think we were surrendering to our fear. Surrendering to the very thing we're trying to prove to them can be defeated."

It took a moment for Shelley to answer, but he was proud of her when she did because she was speaking honestly, speaking from her own issues. "The others—they won't want to... to see me." She cast her eyes down, ashamed to meet his. "How could they bear to look at me, knowing what happened, knowing what I did?"

Her hands were gathered on her knees, like those of a much younger girl fearing chastisement or judgment. He resisted the impulse to reach out his own hand and cover hers, however comforting she may have found it.

"You did nothing wrong," he said. "I'll talk to them all, one on one, ahead of time. I'm completely confident that your fears are unfounded, but I promise you that I'll make sure."

She looked up then, and he was gratified to see that the trust—some of it, at least—had come back into her eyes. He held her gaze for a moment, letting her feel his strength, and then stood up and crossed the room to where the blinds diffused the morning sunlight.

"Oh, and listen, Shelley," he said over his shoulder as he swept the blinds open, letting in the light of day. "I'll also make it clear that anybody who doesn't wish to attend the next session is of course free not to. They're here voluntarily. They're not lab rats." He turned back to face her. "I heard what you said about caring for them as people and I hope you know that I feel the same way. The research aspect of your study is important, very important, and I'd be lying if I pretended I wasn't excited about it—but please don't assume that I ever lose sight of the therapeutic benefits to the patients."

He looked at her as she stood up and gathered her things. "Yes?" he said.

"Yes."

"Yes. We're both on the same page here, Shelley." He made an open-handed gesture and gave a slightly rueful grin. "We're both just doing our best."

Shelley managed a smile for him. It didn't quite reach her eyes, but he appreciated the effort.

8

The quiet days were always a blessing.

It wasn't that Molly Edwards didn't know damned well that silence and stillness in the group study annex room actually meant very little in terms of progress or breakthrough for the kids, knew in fact that it could very often mean the opposite, but quiet was quiet and peace was peace and neither was ever guaranteed in a roomful of special-needs seven-year-olds, so sue her if she chose to enjoy them on those rare and precious occasions when they made an appearance.

She was particularly lucky that the kids were quiet today, with Shelley not coming in and all. Sweet thing had *wanted* to, God bless her, despite the shock of her patient's death, but Molly had told her—stressing that this was her considered professional opinion as a psychologist—that she was batshit fucking crazy if she did and that, should she be stupid enough to show up despite that *pro bono* diagnosis, Molly would personally beat her with a nail-studded stick. And that she better believe she had one. Kept it specially for idiots with an overactive self-sacrifice gene.

Molly was at her desk. Had anybody asked—and she was pretty sure everyone knew her well enough by now to know that they better have some big fucking balls on them to even *think* of asking—she'd have been happy to inform them that she was catching up on some paperwork.

Catching up on some paperwork. The greatest phrase in the entire and glorious history of mind-your-damn-business.

A phrase Molly loved more than she loved her luggage. A phrase that let you avoid lying when you used it—because she was undeniably holding paper in her hand and she was undeniably working her way through it. The fact that the paper constituted the lean and mean *noir*-as-they-come one hundred and ninety-two pages of *Like a Blonde on Heroin* by Jack Martin was nobody's business but hers and her Lord's.

Lookit, if the kids had been at all unresponsive or unhappy when she suggested their making pictures as the morning's activity, she'd have been all over it. If any of them had asked specifically about the reason for Ms. Campbell's absence, she'd have sat them down and talked to them and told them the truth. Not the unpleasant details of what happened to the guy, of course, but that something sad had happened in Ms. Campbell's life and that she needed some time to get through it. And she'd have told them that because, firstly, sad things happen and it did people no good—whether they were seven or seventy—to pretend otherwise and, secondly and even more importantly, you don't fucking lie to children. You can have all the degrees and diplomas in the world, have your bad self a real fancy office and such, but if you didn't embrace *you don't fucking lie to children* as your mantra, as your equivalent of the medical profession's *first do no harm*, then you shouldn't be allowed within two hundred yards of the little bastards.

But in any case, the kids had gone for it. Not a single dissenter in the bunch. Differing degrees of enthusiasm, of course, but any kind of consensus was a minor miracle in this room and Molly wasn't about to run to the Supreme Court to demand a recount. They'd been spread across the room for thirty glorious minutes now, each of them working with their own personal pile of art materials—paper, watercolor paints, brushes, and shit—and damned if all their faces weren't creased not just with concentration but also with something poignantly close to unencumbered happiness as they beavered away on their paintings.

It was true that, at a rough glance, there appeared to be more paint accidentally applied to desks, clothes, faces, and parquet flooring than to paper—and Molly was pretty sure that more than one of the kids had been quietly investigating the nutritional qualities of burnt ocher or aquamarine—but so what? Sorry for the janitorial staff and all, but go ask Jackson Pollock if he gave a rat's ass.

Still, Luke McLaughlin, the terrifying and seemingly indestructible muscle of mob boss Michael Cahill, had just had his nuts sliced off by Kitty Donnelly—who was turning out to be quite the little spitfire—so it was a fine place to take a break in her book. Molly folded down the corner of the next page—Shelley always gave her shit about that, brought her a free bookmark every time she came back from Borders or wherever, but it never took—and stood up in order to take a tour of *Gallerie Ritalin* and check out what masterpieces her miniature Magrittes might have wrought.

Some of the kids—Audrey, Cameron, Mandy—looked up as she started walking toward them, as if eager to lay down their tools and move on to whatever Ms. Edwards might want to do next.

"No, that's alright," Molly said. "You can all keep working on your pictures. I'm just stretching my legs."

Actually, she knew she couldn't push it much longer. An uninterrupted half an hour's concentration on one single activity was an extraordinarily long time for any seven-year-old, with or without ADD, and she was simply delaying the discussion phase out of pure self-protection. Because she was always at a loss as to what to say.

She was fine if they asked her what she *thought* of their pictures. Finding words of praise or encouragement was no problem. How hard was it to fake *that* shit? She'd faked it at gallery openings for eager and talent-free adults, so she was damned sure she could fake it for a bunch of mama's little dividends.

No, what she feared was the other type of question, the direct one, the one about their accuracy of representation: *You know what it is, Ms. Edwards?* Always asked with a glow of excitement in their young eyes and, beneath the false modesty of the question, a quiet confidence that nobody could mistake for anything else what they themselves apparently believed to be a photo-realistic rendering of Grandma's house.

Yeah, that question was much tougher—especially for someone whose mantra was you don't lie to children. Every rule has its exceptions, and Molly knew that replying to the *do you know what it is* question was an exception to that one. Because honesty was utterly out of the question. "Well, sweetie, I'm not really sure, but it appears to be an emphysemic lung getting poked by a bunch of deformed penises," however accurate a description, rarely coincided with the artist's intent and usually resulted in a broken little voice sobbing out "It's my baby brother learning to dance" or some other equally unlikely shit.

She weaved among them, hoping to get a jump on their chosen subject matters, and was both surprised and relieved to see that most of the pictures were actually recognizable. The style of nearly all of them was of course primitive and gestural, but the subjects were pretty apparent, or at least guessable. Reassuringly normal, too—houses, cars, moms, dads, and dogs. Well, one dog. Probably a dog. Tail was the big clue, no matter how much the rest of it looked like a flayed python tottering on evolutionary unlikely Jell-O legs.

No, they'd all done pretty well. Really well. Molly actually looked forward to telling Shelley about their progress.

Taylor Smith, still at that sad and instinctive self-isolating distance from his nearest classmate, was the last child she came to. He'd tucked himself up on his seat, cross-legged and lost in concentration, and was working hard on his picture.

As with the other pictures, Molly had surprisingly little difficulty in seeing what it was that Taylor was painting. In fact, by any objective standard of simple representational ability, his picture was considerably better than those of the others. It even suggested—who knew?—the presence of some genuine incipient talent. There was much to admire in Taylor's execution of his chosen image. The issue was the image itself.

There was what might be a moon in what might be a sky.

If it *was* a moon, it was baring its teeth.

What might be a rope ladder was dangling from it, and what might be a man was descending to Earth.

Most of the elements in the picture were in black and white. But the might-be-a-man was very colorful. Impressionistic slashes of red, green, yellow, and blue covered his body.

Like rags and tatters.

9

"I'm an agoraphobic," Margaret Paris began, once the group was in session, "and have been for as long as I can remember."

She replayed this morning's walk to the campus in her head as she talked. She could see it all quite clearly. She'd trained herself to do that, of course, like fragments shored against her ruin. Each remembered activity that hadn't ended up in crisis or humiliation was one more piece of evidence to set against any future fears. Every time something bad didn't *happen contributed to the fragile but growing body of proof that bad things didn't* always *happen.*

"Mine is a rarer form of the disease, though hardly uncommon," Margaret told the group, finding as ever that a clinical description of her condition in a safe environment was curiously comforting. "It's not crowds that bother me. In fact, crowds help. It's open spaces *without* people that terrify me. The emptiness. The absence. They make me feel naked and alone. And very afraid."

She'd exited her apartment building, patted her pocket to feel the small placebo bulge of the two diazepam pills she carried with her just in case, glanced around—like always—to check that the world hadn't shifted, that she was as usual merely standing outside her building in her busy, built-up part of town, and started to walk.

She'd glanced up constantly at the tall buildings while she walked, as if to reassure herself that they were there and were staying there. But her walk, as ever, had been determined and brisk.

"I've refused, though, to let my affliction turn me into a

recluse," she said. "I've constructed my life carefully to allow me to work around my problem. The building in which I live is seven blocks from the college where I teach—good blocks, solid and busy. My supermarket is five blocks from home, my dentist even nearer."

As she'd reached each corner on her route, she'd paused as she always did—usually briefly these days, thank the Lord—and looked down it as if fearful that the world may have surprised her by disappearing. Only when she'd seen that it hadn't would she turn and continue walking down the next street. There hadn't been any surprises this morning. Well, at least no unpleasant ones. There was one thing she'd thought she better keep track of, though: at one of the bigger intersections on her usual route, a city construction crew had been moving into position. There'd been workers and supervisors in their orange hard hats, the latter waving work trucks into place in the middle of the street, the former placing bright orange cones at the perimeter of the entire area. It would only matter if the whole intersection was going to be closed to pedestrians, so she needed to remember to Google some information tonight and, if necessary, plan some safe and acceptable alternative route until the work was done.

"And I always stick to the same routes when I can," she said. "I don't want any surprises." She paused. "Ever." She'd played the last for a kind of self-knowing, self-mocking effect and was pleased that she won a smile or two from some of the others.

She'd entered the main quad of the college campus and headed not for her own department but for the building that was home to Drayton and Shelley's project. Crossing the building's lobby to the bank of elevators, she'd seen that one of them, already filled to near capacity with students and faculty, was about to close its door. She'd rushed forward and squeezed her way in, with suitably apologetic smiles to her sardine neighbors.

"Most people hate a crowded elevator," she said. "I always feel lucky to find one. Today was lucky."

Shelley Campbell was sitting next to her in the group study room and, as Margaret finished speaking, Shelley reached out and gave her hand a small squeeze of reassurance and support. Or just affection. Margaret gave her a small smile of gratitude in return and found herself thinking, not for the first time, that though Alex Drayton might be the senior man here, he could learn a lot about bedside manner from this one.

The good doctor himself was standing behind Shelley and Margaret's chairs, ready to start the session proper, and Sarah and Richie, each in their own chairs within the semicircle, were busy being silent and attentive. That new fellow, Tom Lawson—Margaret wasn't entirely sure she liked him—he was being attentive, too, but in a slightly different way. Margaret didn't really care for the way his eyes were so much more... *active*... than those of the others, the way they flicked constantly around the room, as if taking in every possible detail. He seemed particularly fascinated, in what Margaret would have sworn was an almost macabrely amused way, by the presence of another chair, set off slightly to the side of the group. For absent friends. There was a framed photograph of Anthony Esposito on it, along with flowers and a small wreath.

With an unobtrusive cough, Drayton called them back to order and, at his urging, Margaret and Shelley each leaned back in their chairs, tilted their heads even further back, and closed their eyes.

Drayton began rubbing gently at Margaret's temples. "Alright," he said. "Let's find our quiet place. You're safe.

MOONTOWN

You're surrounded by love. Your breathing is easy and free..."

Margaret felt her body relaxing even more into the chair and sensed Shelley's doing the same beside her.

"A friend is with you, Margaret," Drayton said. "She won't let anything harm you..."

Shelley's hand reached out and enfolded Margaret's.

"...and both of you are in a safe place. A place where nothing can hurt you and therefore a place where nothing need be forgotten or denied." He paused briefly to let her mind begin to process that and, when he spoke again, his voice was even quieter and more gentle. "Tell us where you are, Margaret.

"A safe place," Margaret heard herself say softly and sleepily.

"And what do you see?"

For a tiny dislocating second Margaret could almost feel her own eyes moving REM-like beneath her closed lids, but that wasn't what she was seeing, that wasn't where she was...

Again, somebody far away asked her, "What do you see?"

"Flowers..." said a very distant voice that sounded a little like hers.

*

A score of colorful wild blossoms filled Margaret's sight.

Her face must have been pressed very close to the flowers. Barely visible through their thousand petals there was a rolling green field in the distance beyond.

Margaret could hear things, too. She could hear a babbling brook and a summer breeze. She could hear the excited whispers of children.

What she couldn't do right now was remember where she was or what she was doing. But that was alright. The day was lovely and…

The wild blossoms swayed in the gentle wind, brushing her mouth and nose.

Oh, she was so silly.

What did she mean she couldn't remember where she was?

She was in the woods behind the field. She was with her friends. They were having a wonderful time. Her name was Margaret Paris and she was eight years old and right now she was crouching behind a big old tree because it was her turn to go seek.

She could hear them now, hear her five friends rushing off in various directions. She could look if she wanted, but she wasn't going to because that would be cheating.

"You'll never find us!" Jamie shouted from somewhere deeper in the woods. Margaret smiled to herself. She wasn't stupid. If he was shouting from the woods he was trying to trick her. He and the others would double back. They'd be out in the field.

Margaret put her hands over her eyes. "Five…ten…fifteen," she said aloud, in case they were checking, "twenty…twenty-five…thirty…"

*

In the group study room, Alex Drayton looked at the closed eyes of the two women and listened to the sound of their breathing.

Margaret had been counting aloud. Shelley's mouth had been opening and closing in time with hers.

"It's later now," Alex said. "What do you see?"

There was silence for a moment, and then a small unconscious whimper of anxiety from Margaret.

Moontown

"What do you see?" he said again.

*

Margaret, who hadn't found her friends yet, was walking out from the wooded area into the big open field. She liked the way the wild grass swayed in the summer breeze, liked the way it brushed against her and tickled her, even though it was almost tall enough to reach her chin.

"You're not in the woods!" she shouted out, sure that her friends could hear her. "I'll find you!"

She began to run, rushing into the middle of the field and sweeping at the grass with her hands, as if to force her friends out of hiding.

"I'll find you!" she shouted again.

The light grew suddenly dim, very dim indeed, and Margaret gasped in surprise.

She looked up to see that, overhead, a heavy gray cloud had drifted over the sun.

That was alright, she supposed, but it was funny that, along with the dimming of the light, there had come a sudden and thorough silence.

The whistling of the wind, the buzzing of the insects, the twittering of the birds had all ceased instantly and completely. Margaret had been to see an orchestra once, in the big concert hall, and remembered how the man in the front — he was called the conductor — had brought down his stick — it was called a baton — in one sweeping move and how everybody had stopped playing all at the same time. This was like that. As if a conductor that she couldn't see had brought down his invisible baton and all the sounds of the world had stopped.

Margaret's eyes flicked back across the tall grass, the endless tall grass, as if hoping this change in circumstance would bring her friends out to join her.

Her voice sounded funny when it was the only sound in the world.

"Mikey?" she said. "Susan? Jamie?"

There was no movement. No reply. No sound at all.

All that happened was that the darkness grew in intensity and oppression. It felt like a thunderstorm was coming, or something worse. Margaret looked out and around herself at the vast open field…

…and, terrifyingly, the emptiness began to increase itself.

The woods, the horizon, everything that wasn't flat and empty and awful seemed to recede from her, leaving her alone, truly and appallingly alone, as if she were literally miles from any break in the flat and darkening landscape.

She felt her face crumble into something fearful and ready to cry. Pathetically, she called out one last time for her vanished friends.

"Where are you?!"

Nothing.

Shrinking into herself, her head sinking between her hunching shoulders and her hands gripping her elbows, she forced herself to look up again, to look directly overhead. The dim outline of the sun was shrinking and receding, as if it too was flying away from her, or she was falling away from it.

She was alone in a terrible place now, a dim gray void of a universe that was silent and empty.

And then the moon rose.

It was huge and swollen, and it rose preternaturally fast over the horizon, expanding impossibly to almost fill the sky as it slid across the darkness into dominance overhead.

Margaret hunkered down further, feeling like she was being squashed by this monster moon. She looked at it again and what she saw this time made her scream.

Because the moon's surface was crawling into life. The shadows and darknesses of its craters and gulleys were shimmering and slithering, and sliding together into a nightmare version of facial features.

Moontown

The Man in the Moon was looking at her.

That's what other people called him, but Margaret knew his real name. She'd heard it on her parent's radio and she hadn't liked it.

Mister Moonlight.

Daddy had laughed when Margaret had told him she was afraid of Mister Moonlight. He'd told her that Mister Moonlight was friendly, that that's what it said in the song. But Margaret had known better, because as soon as she'd heard the name she'd seen him in her head and he hadn't looked friendly at all.

She realized now that she'd always known he'd come for her one day. And now he had.

Mister Moonlight was grinning at her and his grin was just as mean and cruel as she'd expected. Sobbing in terror, she threw her hands across her face. But she couldn't make herself close her eyes and, through her fingers, she could still see what was happening.

Mister Moonlight was peeling himself free from the moon like a snail from its shell and his eyes were very excited as he prepared to descend from the sky and claim her.

Margaret bowed her head because she didn't want to see anymore and she stretched her little arms upward in a hopeless attempt to keep him away, feeling her fingers strain and stretch in tension and fear.

And then a hand grabbed her wrist.

"No!" Margaret screamed, though she wished she hadn't. He might answer her and she couldn't bear to imagine what the sound of his voice would be like, the sound of cold and bone-white rock. But that wasn't the sound she heard.

"It's alright…" said a lady's voice. "It's alright, Margaret. I've got you."

Hardly daring to hope, almost certain that this was just one of Mister Moonlight's cruel tricks, Margaret looked up.

The field was normal again.

PETER ATKINS

The cloud had gone from the sun. The tall grass was swaying in the wind.

And a pretty young woman was holding Margaret's hand safely in hers and was helping her to her feet.

"I've got you," the lady said again...

*

...and, still gasping in remembered terror, Margaret opened her eyes in the group study room.

Shelley still had hold of her hand, and now put her other arm around Margaret's shoulder.

"Oh my God," said Margaret, blinking in confusion and looking around the room, seeing Drayton, seeing the others, realizing—slowly—that she was safe.

"Are you okay?" Shelley asked. Probably not for the first time, Margaret thought, but she still couldn't quite use her voice to answer. She met Shelley's eyes, though, and gave a nod. Small and cautious, maybe, but a nod.

"Everything's all right, Margaret," said Alex Drayton, and Margaret was surprised to feel a tiny and instinctive voice inside her wanting to snap at him, *how the fuck would you know?* She regretted the feeling, because she knew that he didn't intend anything more than a reassurance, but there was something in that tone of his, a confidence that seemed to her both misplaced and arrogant.

The others, Margaret saw, were staring almost transfixed at Shelley and her. Especially Tom Lawson. "Didn't *sound* like everything was all right," he said.

Margaret ignored him, ignored them all really, and kept her eyes on Shelley. "I never remembered..." she said, and she heard in her own voice a mix of confusion and...was that really *optimism*? Yes, she realized. Yes, it was. Tremulous and cautious, perhaps, but actually there.

"What happened?" Shelley asked her. "That day, I mean. Did you find your friends?"

Margaret nodded. "Yes," she said. "It was nothing. I see that now. Nothing. A cloud over the sun. A scared little girl's imagination." She felt her face begin to crumble. "My God, all those years..."

The tears came then, but marvelously they were tears of regret for the past and not of fear for the future. She relaxed into them, allowing herself to be pulled closer into Shelley's comforting embrace.

10

Shelley had two hundred channels available on her TV.

She had no idea why because she certainly didn't pay for them. Yeah, like that was affordable for a postgrad, even one on a research grant. They were just there, as the landlord had claimed they would be when she'd apartment-hunted the place months earlier. "And free cable!" he'd said, with no further explanation. Shelley'd known not to ask any questions, known that someone in one of the four-plex's apartments *was* paying for the service and that someone else, probably a technically and criminally proficient friend of the landlord, had hot-wired the system to send it into the other three units.

Anyway, the point was not that she had two hundred channels legally or otherwise available to her but how astonishing it was that that wide range of choices still regularly left her without anything she actually felt like watching.

She hadn't even bothered curling herself into the big armchair that faced the TV, just stood behind it and speed-thumbed her remote through the channel guide—*and, by the way, just how many documentaries about Hitler could one world produce? Was it like a fucking* contest *or something?*—and then killed the screen, tossed the remote onto the chair, and headed for the bedroom to retrieve her iPod from the pile of her jogging clothes. She'd dock it in the mini stereo system and let Radio Shelley keep her company while she transcribed her notes about the day's session with Margaret.

She wasn't even aware that she'd glanced over at the shelf

unit above and behind the TV until she stopped walking and turned back to look at it more consciously.

Her passing glance—perhaps not even a glance, perhaps just peripheral vision—had told her that there was something wrong there, that something was out of place. It hadn't done anything so useful as to tell her what it *was*, of course, had merely set her spider-sense tingling.

She looked more carefully across the shelves and their haphazard collections of books, ornaments, and CDs—*Oh yeah, CDs. Remember them? CD, meet eight-track and vinyl, you guys will have a lot to talk about*—and tried to find whatever it was that had bothered her.

Her gaze settled on the lowest shelf—all books apart from the stupid and kitschy little Elvis bust that Jen had brought her back from a day trip to Tijuana—and she knew that she was getting warmer. She narrowed her focus to the spines of the books…

And there it was. A wrong *color*, or at least a color in the wrong place, that was what had caught her eye. Fitted snugly between the familiar orange of a Penguin Classic and the pretentious faux-leather of a book of poems-for-people-who-don't-actually-read-poetry was a tall thin volume with a spine of bright yellow.

Shelley felt a sudden and unfocused stab of fear. She didn't understand it for a second or two, not until she realized that she recognized the book and that the fear was the kind of sense-memory response that would have given old Ivan Pavlov a real hard-on.

It was a book from her childhood, one that her mother used to read to her until she'd been old enough to read it for herself. She wondered what it was that had suddenly made its familiar and nearly twenty-year-old spine seem odd and out of place enough to nibble at her attention after all this time.

And then she had a stranger thought. It *wasn't* that it had suddenly caught her eye after months of just standing invisibly amongst its neighboring books. She really didn't remember her copy of the book ever being on this shelf. Or anywhere in the apartment, come to that. She wasn't even sure that it had ever left her parents' house. Why *would* she have brought it with her? She hadn't liked it very much.

It was called *Jenny and the Dark* and it was written by somebody with what she now found to be the unlikely name of Wilfred Tibble. She'd had a different opinion about Mister Tibble's name when she was a little girl, she remembered. It had unsettled her. Quite a lot. *It's not a man's name, Mommy*, she'd said. *It's a cat's name.* Tibble. Like a tabby or like Mister Tibbs, the cat in that movie about the dogs. She'd pictured the author in her imagination, pictured him as a small, shrunken elderly man in an old-fashioned black jacket-with-tails but with, between his weak old man's shoulders, the human-size head of a far from weak and far from old gray and black tabby cat.

It could have been a cute image in the hands of the right illustrator, Shelley supposed now, but it hadn't been the slightest bit cute in her childhood imagining, primarily because of Mister Tibble's eyes. They'd been fully feline and glintingly alive with an atavistic predatory coldness, as if Mister Tibble knew that all little girls were mice and that he could play with them whenever he wanted.

But it wasn't only her accidental and presumably inaccurate vision of the book's creator that Shelley's younger self had been afraid of. The book itself—not the *object*, of course, but rather the story-in-verse that it contained—had frightened her as well. Come to think of it, though, that too had been partly the fault of her own imagination. She'd misheard the title the first time her mother had read it aloud and had thought it the name of the story's comic villain—who was not, after all, so comic when you were four years old and suggestible. She hadn't heard *Jenny and the Dark*, but instead *Johnny in the Dark*, and the picture she'd involuntarily made of *him* had made Mister Tibble look like a kid's best friend.

No, wait a minute. That wasn't entirely right.

Shelley felt her memory shifting and sorting, revealing another layer of itself, one that had lain undisturbed for the same two decades that the book had remained unopened.

It wasn't as simple as her younger self having misheard the title. It was the dream. The dream had told it to her that way.

*

Knockity-knock-knock-knock.

That's the sound they hear, Shelley and her mom, the sound of someone making a big production number out of knocking at their front door.

Shelley doesn't like the sound and pretends not to hear it. She knows that it's late. She knows that it's dark outside and she doesn't want the door to be opened.

Knockity-knock-knock-knock.

Shelley and her mom are watching TV. They're watching something Mom likes. Mom likes really old movies. Not just old, *really* old. Not just movies from before there were colors in the world, but movies from back before people had learned to talk.

"This is called slapstick", Mom has said when they've watched similar things before. *Slapstick*. Shelley doesn't like the sound of that. She's a good girl and has never been spanked or slapped, but she bets it hurts more with a stick. The show they're watching now seems much meaner than the other ones Shelley has seen, as if this is what slapstick does when it thinks the teacher isn't looking. There were two men. One of them was big and one of them was little. They wore clothes that were baggy and dusty, and their faces were very white as if they were dusty too. But the black lines around their eyes had hard dark edges. They'd come back to see a butcher who had cheated them out of some money and they had done awful things to his shop and were now setting about doing awful things to him.

"Aren't they *silly?*" Mom says to Shelley, with the big happy smile she uses when she wants Shelley to believe something that isn't true. Shelley doesn't think the men are silly; she thinks the men are mean and crazy, and she watches disapprovingly as they feed the butcher who'd stolen their money into his own mincing machine, the littler one laughing silently as the sausages come out while the larger one stares right out of the screen at them, winking and nodding and putting his thumb up in the air.

Knockity-knock-knock-knock.

As if the knocking itself is the trigger of the memory, Shelley suddenly remembers that tonight is Halloween and that unannounced visitors aren't necessarily unusual.

But there's still something about the sound of that knock —the sound of its *insistence*—that she doesn't like and she's not very happy when Mom stands up without a word and starts walking toward the front door.

Moontown

Mom hasn't told Shelley to come with her but Shelley thinks perhaps she better, and she catches up to Mom just as she opens the door.

Shelley wonders when the streetlights went out and why it's only the light of the moon that shines on the two people who are standing on their front porch.

For some reason, Mom doesn't seem to recognize them straight away. But Shelley does. They are the men they've just been watching, the men from Slapstick. They are sort of in color now, though they're doing their best to pretend that they aren't; their various pieces of clothing are either black or white or gray and their faces are covered with thick white stuff. Shelley supposes the white stuff is make-up, like Mom wears sometimes, but it's powdery and lumpy and looks like it wouldn't feel nice to wear or to touch. Somewhere between where they came from and their arrival at Shelley's front door, the men have learned to talk.

"Oh look, Mister Ess," says the bigger one, "a customer."

The littler one smiles. "*Two* customers, Mister Ess," he says, and his eyes flick from Shelley to her mom and back again. "A Major and a Minor."

"Standard and Economy sizes, as it were," says the first.

"Full-strength and Concentrated," says the second, nodding in agreement.

"Regular and Condensed."

"Condensed," the smaller one says admiringly. "Oh, Mister Ess, you've hit it precisely! *Condensed*. Just add water."

"Before you throw it in the pan."

And then they both look at Shelley and laugh, like they've just made a hilarious joke. Shelley remembers what they did to the butcher on TV and doesn't think the joke is very funny.

She reaches her hand quietly up toward her mom's but Mom doesn't notice and Shelley doesn't make a fuss because she doesn't want to draw even more attention from the men.

Why isn't Mom bothered by these people, Shelley wonders? It isn't only that they're from the TV but that they're *grown-ups*. And that isn't right at all. Halloween visitors are supposed to be children. It's not… what's that word?… *appropriate* for grown-ups to be out knocking on people's doors and looking for candy. And Shelley finds their clothes and their make-up scary in a way that isn't fun-scary like the masks and the costumes worn by the neighborhood kids, even the older ones. These men aren't playing let's-pretend. This is who they truly are.

"New to the neighborhood, Madam," says the bigger one to Shelley's mom. "Introducing ourselves, as it were."

"As surprised to be here," says the smaller one, "as you are, no doubt, surprised to see us."

The bigger one nods. "For what unlikely twist of a benevolent fate," he says, "what curious whim of the gods of comic happenstance, would have deposited upon your humble and—no offense, Madam—singularly unprepossessing doorstep, the likes of us."

Shelley hears how proud the big man sounds when he says *the likes of us* and, when Mom doesn't say anything, when neither she nor Shelley clap, the little one cocks his head as if surprised. "The uncrowned Kings of Vaudeville," he says. "And the newly celebrated sensations of the silver screen."

"Mister Sponge…" says the big one, gesturing at his friend.

"…and Mister Scrotum," says the little one, gesturing back.

Moontown

"Two who should never be strangers," they say together, and they both bow at the same time.

Shelley is all at once very aware of the question that the men haven't asked. She doesn't really want to say it for them, but something makes her feel like she has to. Perhaps asking it will make everything go more quickly.

"Trick or treat?" she says.

The two men—*are* they men, Shelley suddenly wonders? Because the baggy and grimy white shirt beneath the dusty black jacket of the bigger one seems as if it might be trying to hide Mom-size breasts—look at each other in response to Shelley's question and Shelley doesn't like the mutual eager glint that comes into their eyes, especially when it's turned back to look again at her and Mom.

"Trick or treat," says Mister Scrotum, as if trying the words out in his mouth and deciding he likes them. "*Trick or treat.* Oh, a little of both I'd say, Mister Ess. How about you?"

"Smidgen of each, Mister Ess," says Mister Sponge, nodding thoughtfully. "Smidgen of each."

Though they appear to be addressing each other, their black-outlined eyes remain fixed on Shelley and her mom.

"But first," says Mister Scrotum, raising a finger, "some business. A matter of no pressing urgency, but it never hurts to take care of these things should opportunity deign to present itself. We can't help but find ourselves wondering, Lady and Small Companion, if by any chance our dear friend Nell has been by this way before our own arrival?" He twists his head a little, trying to look past Shelley and her mom into their house's hallway. "Might, in fact, have left something for us?"

"A jar," says Mister Sponge. "With contents."

Mister Scrotum has only said *Nell*, but when his friend says *jar* Shelley knows exactly who it is that they're talking about. She knows that Nell is short for Eleanor, whose last name is Rigby and who is the monster in that old song that her mom likes. Shelley knows that Nell Rigby is a monster because Nell Rigby wears a face that she keeps in a jar by the door.

Shelley stops herself from turning to look at the hallstand. She doesn't want to look, because she is afraid that the jar will in fact be there, is afraid that something pale and moist will be floating in its oily water. She doesn't look. She doesn't even twitch her eyes. But Mister Sponge winks at her anyway, like he knows precisely what she was thinking, like they have a secret now, a special secret that makes them friends.

"No, I'm sorry," says Mom. "You're the first tonight."

"Really?" says Mister Scrotum. "I find myself most surprised by that morsel of information. Don't you, Mister Ess? Find yourself surprised by that?"

"Surprised?" says Mister Sponge. "Not been this astonished since my last plate of *steak tartare* turned out to be a juggler I'd once worked with at the Palace of Varieties in Cedar Rapids, Iowa."

"Not Rodney 'Magic Hands' Russell?" asks Mister Scrotum.

"The very same, Sir," says Mister Sponge. "A most amusing fellow as you no doubt recall, Mister Ess, with a nice line in plate-spinning. Tasted like dehydrated camel."

Mister Scrotum looks down at Shelley. "First tonight, are we?" he says. "Not even a quick visit from your friend Johnny in the Dark?"

Shelley shakes her head, no. "I don't know him," she says,

and tells herself that that's the truth. Even though, like before, she immediately knows who he means.

Mister Sponge looks at her too. "Well, that is indeed passing strange, my little miniature," he says. "Because he certainly knows you." He turns to his partner. "Speaks most fondly of her, does he not, Mister Ess?"

"Like they're the oldest and dearest of acquaintances," says Mister Scrotum, but he says it like someone who is already growing bored with that particular topic and he snaps his fingers by his own face as if suddenly remembering more important business. He beams at Shelley and her mother as if whatever comes next is sure to be fun.

"Here's the thing, Missus and Midget," he says. "Whether they find themselves on the finest stages of the Orpheum circuit or in these most miserable and reduced of circumstances, Mister Sponge and Mister Scrotum hold only one truth to be self-evident." He pauses for a second, as if ready to receive guesses. When none are forthcoming, he continues: "And what truth is that, Mister Ess?"

"That the show," says Mister Sponge, "must go on."

"That the show must go on," says Mister Scrotum, and his eyes are alight with joy. "So what shall it be?" he asks, his gaze not leaving Shelley and her mom. "A mimetic representation of the sundering of Babylon's great wall? Or perhaps the comic dialogue we like to call *How the Green Death Came to the Palace of the Khan*, with balloon animals?"

"For we have been princes in different kingdoms," says Mister Sponge in a stranger voice, "and our memory is as long as our talents are timeless."

"Though I wonder, Block and Chip," says Mister Scrotum as if his partner hadn't spoken, "if it might not after all be our soft-shoe and black-face interpretation of the Stations of the Cross that would most float your boats and bob your barnacles?"

He raises a questioning eyebrow at Shelley's mom.

"No?" he says, without really giving her time to answer. "How about this, then?"

And then he drives his hand through her mother's chest and pulls out her heart.

*

It wasn't like Shelley had ever forgotten the dream—it had terrified her poor younger self for weeks and she'd needed to sleep with her bedroom lights on for more than a month—but eventually, like most childhood nightmares, it had lost its power over her and dwindled into something that was rarely remembered and even then merely in snatches and highlights.

Her lifelong distaste for slapstick was undeniably stronger than the usual *chicks don't dig the Stooges* shit, but she'd managed to sit freakout-free through a Buster Keaton double feature at the Beverly Theater a couple years back at the urging of a guy she was way into. "Keaton isn't *slapstick*," he'd insisted, "and he's got none of Chaplin's sentimentality—Buster isn't about pathos, he's about the freezing touch of melancholia." *The freezing touch of melancholia.* Wow. She'd been certain he was just quoting someone—and without attribution at that—but it had got him to second base in a fucking heartbeat. Chicks don't dig the Stooges, but they do dig the poetic pretty boys. At least chicks called Shelley Campbell.

What she *hadn't* remembered from the dream was that it was those creepy powder-faced bastards—*Mister Sponge?*

Moontown

Mister Scrotum? *Where the hell had she heard* that *word at four years old?*—who'd planted that Johnny in the Dark misnomer in her head.

Anyway, the book was creepy enough to her even without the malapropic assistance of nightmare vaudevillians, so it was time to put it back in a less prominent place in her bookcase. Or throw it up on eBay right now and let it fuck with someone else's childhood.

Shelley had only intended to move *Jenny and the Dark* further along the shelf, but the feel of it as she pulled it out from between the other two books gave her pause. There was something odd about the way her fingers closed around it, something about the book that felt swollen, as if its belly was bloated or distended. She tilted it up to look at it more closely.

There was something inside it. Not actually within the pages but tucked between the dust jacket and the book itself. She was about to reach up inside the jacket to grab at whatever it was, but suddenly found herself fearful of what her fingers might make contact with—fearful that maybe something disgusting had crawled up there and died. A large insect, perhaps, or a small rodent. Before she could psych herself out further, she lifted the book upright and pulled the jacket away from the spine, allowing enough slack between them to let the hidden object fall out onto the shelf.

It was nothing creepy or weird, thank Christ. In fact, it was kind of cool. Shelley picked it up in order to have a better look at it.

It was a matchbook, a vintage one. And one that had obviously been looked after—its bright yellow background undimmed by time. Something from at least the nineteen-thirties, she guessed, judging by the graphics—*what did they call that style? Streamline Moderne, wasn't it?*—and the art deco lettering.

Moonglow Supper Room, that lettering read, above the stylized renderings of tuxedoed nightclubbers having themselves a Gatsby of a time. And then, below the picture: *Cocktails. Dancing.*

Shelley liked it, wherever it had been hiding. It was like a message from history, a calling card from a long-dead past. She propped it up against the Elvis bust. She was almost sorry she didn't smoke.

11

It was way past Taylor Smith's bedtime.

He didn't think he'd ever been up this late. He knew he'd never been *out* this late.

He'd thought there'd be grown-ups around. They didn't have to go to bed when they were told, so why would they? He'd thought he'd have to hide, to wait till the grown-ups weren't looking, and sneak his way past them to where he was going. But that wasn't the case at all.

The campus was completely deserted.

Apart from the moon, the only light on the quad and the buildings surrounding it came from the two big lights. The two big lights were mounted high on the side of the tallest wall. Taylor knew they were called security lights, because he'd heard Ms. Campbell call them that. But their light was white and cold, and it didn't make him feel secure. Their light had hard edges, and outside those edges the dark was just as dark.

Taylor stood still for a moment, feeling the emptiness, listening to the silence, looking at the darkness.

He understood something now.

When grown-ups talked about midnight, he'd always thought it was a time, a place on the clock like any other. But it wasn't.

This was what they meant by midnight. This feeling.

He understood something else, as well. This was why people went to sleep. It wasn't because they were tired. It was to hide from this quiet and lonely darkness. Taylor wanted to hide, too.

But he had something to do first, and so he set off across the quad.

All the doors he needed to be open were open, just like he'd been told they would be. The last door was to his classroom, and that was unlocked too. Taylor creaked it open and looked inside. The classroom looked different in the dark, but the silver-blue moonlight that came in through the windows on the other side of the room was light enough for Taylor to see the thing in the middle of the room.

He'd tried to stop their building it, but they must have come back without him and finished the job because the playhouse was completed now. Its red plastic roof was firmly attached to its yellow plastic walls, and the front wall had been fitted with its red plastic door. Taylor thought it was funny—and not funny ha-ha—that its red and its yellow were so bright and clear. The moonlight didn't do that to the other things in the room. It hid their colors—washed them out, like it was letting them sleep—but it brought the playhouse's colors to a bright glowing life.

Taylor stood in the classroom's open doorway for quite a long time, keeping his fingers on the door handle. He didn't think anything was going to happen that would make him need to slam the door quickly, but he wasn't completely sure. He'd put a quilted jacket on over his pajamas, and his other arm pulled it tighter around his body. He didn't really know why he did that. It wasn't like he was cold or anything. After a while, he felt his sockless feet twitch inside his Heelies, as if they didn't like standing still anymore, and so he let them lead him inside the room.

He left the door halfway open behind him and looked carefully at all the darkened corners of the room as he made his way over to the playhouse. He stopped a couple of feet from its red plastic door and moved his head from side to side and up and down. He knew that he couldn't really check out the playhouse the way his favorite robot would, that the movements of his head weren't really providing night-vision and infra-red scans to his central computer to be compared against a database of all known defense systems, but it made him feel better to pretend that he could. He even did his best imitation of the metallic whirring noise that accompanied DB101's telescoping scanners. But he didn't like how his robot voice echoed in the empty room and so he stopped.

As confidently as he could, he stepped forward and pulled open the plastic front door. He moved inside the snug confines of the playhouse's single room and closed the door behind him.

Inside the yellow room, there were two red plastic chairs and one small yellow plastic table. On the table, there was a red plastic telephone. Taylor, surprised that he didn't need to crouch to keep his head clear of the playhouse's ceiling, moved further in and sat down in one of the chairs. He stared across the tiny space and out of the playhouse's single window. It wasn't really a *window*, Taylor thought, it was just a round hole in the playhouse wall. But through it he could see the shadowy moonlit classroom. That made him feel kind of good and he decided he'd sit there a while and keep looking at it.

The little plastic telephone rang.

It was loud and it was sudden and Taylor jerked in shock. He looked down at the phone on the table and his brow creased in confusion. *It's a* toy *phone*, he said to himself, *it can't ring on its own.*

It rang again.

Rather than lift the handset, Taylor picked the whole phone up and looked at it carefully. It was two pieces of molded plastic. There was no jack. There was no cord. It wasn't a phone.

It rang again.

Taylor picked up the plastic handset and put it to his ear. "Hello?" he said.

A grown-up's voice answered. It was a man's voice and it didn't say hello or tell Taylor who it was. It knew who *he* was, though. "Look out the window, Taylor," it said.

Without thinking, Taylor did what the voice told him to and looked up from the phone and through the playhouse window again.

But he wasn't looking out at the classroom anymore.

Taylor didn't hear himself gasp, but he thought that he must have because of the strange sound that the voice at the other end of the line made as if in response. It was a very little sound, one that Taylor could hardly hear, but he didn't like it very much. Taylor didn't have a dog but his Aunt Lisa did, and the sound reminded him of the sound of Prince's tongue lapping eagerly and hungrily at something that had been carelessly spilled.

Through the window, Taylor was looking at what appeared to be an exterior landscape. A narrow country road wound far away between dark hills. There were no stars at all. Taylor remembered how he'd felt earlier, remembered that midnight feeling, and knew that he was looking now into the place where midnight lived.

Far back along the twisting road, too far away for Taylor to read what may have been written on it, there was an old wooden signpost. After a moment, it began to sway as if an angry wind was making its way towards him from whatever place it was that that road led to.

"Uh-oh," said the voice on the phone, "something's coming."

Taylor couldn't look away from the window onto the midnight world. He kept watching as, in the distance, a shadow appeared over the crest of the road. He kept watching as the shadow grew and kept growing.

"Something's coming," the voice repeated. "Something bad."

Taylor whimpered in fear and once again felt the voice at the other end somehow lick up his fear like a thirsty animal before it continued to speak.

"Do you know what it is that's coming, Taylor?" it said.

Taylor's voice was tiny and frightened. "What...what is it?" he said.

"It's *me*," said the voice. And then it began to laugh. It was not a nice laugh.

Taylor slammed the handset back down on the phone. He didn't want to talk to that man anymore. He was very frightened and he wanted to run away. But the window of the playhouse was on the same side as the front door, and he knew that if he opened the door, he'd be running toward the big shadow of the bad thing that was coming for him or at the very least showing it where he was. He looked around the little plastic room, knowing there was nowhere to hide and telling himself not to cry.

There was another door in the back wall of the playhouse. Taylor stared at it for a second. He knew that it hadn't been there before. He knew that it was a magic door, but he didn't know if it was good magic or bad magic. He didn't know what would be on the other side.

He looked back at the window and wished that he hadn't. The shadow was much nearer now and moving faster. Everything it passed over stayed just as dark as the shadow itself, as if nothing could ever come out from under the shadow once it had been touched by it.

Taylor knew that he mustn't let the shadow touch him, that nothing could be worse than that. He yanked open the door in the back wall of the playhouse and ran through it.

He almost fell down the stairs because he hadn't expected them to be there, but he found his footing and raced down them, hardly taking time to be surprised that they were made of the same brightly colored plastic as the playhouse itself. The staircase was steep but not long and within seconds Taylor was at the bottom of it and running along the narrow corridor to which it led. The corridor was made of plastic too, and Taylor had to run carefully because its shiny yellow floor was slippery.

There was another red plastic door at the end of the corridor and Taylor ran towards it. He didn't look back, not once, because he could hear behind him the echoing sounds of something big and strong pounding down the stairs and he knew that if he looked back he would not be able to see the stairs at all, would see only the shadow as it swallowed them up one by one.

He heard the sounds change and knew that the shadow had reached the other end of the corridor. He ran faster, ran as fast as he dared, and when he reached the red door he didn't stop to think at all, just pulled it open and ran through.

He ran three more steps without even looking, before the surprise of seeing where he was made him stop.

Moontown

Somehow, he was outside, in the open night air.

But he wasn't outside the classroom and he wasn't outside the campus. He was in a place he didn't think he'd ever seen before.

It was a park. A tiny park, a kid-size park. A children's playground, really. There were climbing frames and swings and there were lots of sandboxes. Taylor was standing right in front of one of the sandboxes. All of them—the frames, the swings, the sandboxes—were set on grassy hills. The hills were tiny. Toy-town hills, hills built for kids. The whole of the park was surrounded by a low metal fence as if it was a special place set aside for children. Taylor thought that perhaps it only looked odd because he'd never been in a kid's playground at night, never seen one lit only by the moon.

It was funny, too, that the moon seemed to be shining only on the playground itself. Beyond the perimeter fence, any surrounding landscape was lost in darkness. Just inside one stretch of the fence there was a big painted sign. Taylor knew how to read, and he read what the sign said. It said:

JIMMY MIDNIGHT'S GARDEN OF DELIGHTS.

Taylor stood and stared at the sign for a moment before remembering, with a sudden stab of fear, that he hadn't closed the red door behind him. He turned back to close it, but he couldn't because the door wasn't there anymore. There was no door, no corridor, and no stairs. There was nothing between Taylor and the nearest stretch of fence, nothing at all to show him how he had come to the playground, and nothing to show him the way back.

From behind him—from the sandbox he'd been nearest to—he heard a strange sound. It was a clicking sound. *Click-click-click.* Like a cartoon crab clicking its claws.

Taylor suddenly had a picture in his head and it was a picture of crabs, lots and lots of crabs, crawling out from their hiding places beneath the sand in all of the sandboxes. It wasn't a nice picture because the crabs weren't cartoon crabs at all. He jumped back around quickly to reassure himself that the picture wasn't true. And it wasn't. There were no crabs.

But Taylor was no longer alone.

Two small figures were crouched in the sandbox directly in front of him. At first they had their backs to Taylor but, as if they could tell he was looking at them, they stood up and turned to face him.

It was a little boy and a little girl.

Taylor wondered if they were a brother and a sister, because they looked very much like each other.

They were both very pale, and they both had very black hair. Their hair was very long, and so were their fingernails.

Taylor had never seen fingernails so long. Each nail was longer than the finger from which it grew. Quite a lot longer.

The little boy and the little girl held their hands upright in front of their chests, palms inward, as if they thought Taylor might not have noticed their fingernails and they wanted to give him a chance to see them properly.

The little boy clicked two of the nails of his left hand against each other. *Click-click-click*. But he didn't look at his nails. Like his sister, he was only looking at Taylor.

"They kept growing..." said the little girl.

"...after we died," said the little boy.

"And nobody comes to cut them," said the little girl.

"Will *you* cut them?" said the little boy.

Taylor just stared blankly at the little dead children, not having anything to say.

Moontown

The little girl cocked her head, as if trying to understand Taylor's silence. "Do you not have *scissors*?" she said.

Taylor still didn't speak, but he managed to shake his head to indicate that, no, he didn't have scissors.

The little boy spoke again, and this time there was a tiny hope in his voice. "Perhaps *he* has scissors," he said.

"Who?" said Taylor.

"Your friend," said the little girl.

"The one you brought here with you," the little boy said, and his eyes flicked across to the space immediately behind Taylor.

The fear felt like ice forming in his chest as Taylor turned around to see who it was that had come here with him.

The man towered over Taylor. He was tall, very tall indeed, so tall that Taylor thought he might have been on stilts inside his jet-black pants. He was leaning down, though, so that his head could be closer to Taylor and so that Taylor could see his smile. His smile made Taylor want to cry. The man had a hat that was tall and black and shiny, like people had in pictures from the olden days, and he was wearing it at a tilted angle as if he thought that was funny or clever. His face was white as snow and his eyes were black as coal. His snug-fitting and long-tailed coat was black too, and pinned on its lapel was a big round button with words formed from bright and jolly letters in many colors.

HELLO CHILDREN, it said. *I'M JIMMY MIDNIGHT!!*

Jimmy Midnight had nothing to say to Taylor. Instead, he simply flung his arms wide and lifted them high, like he was flaring an invisible cape. But it wasn't a cape and it wasn't invisible for long. Darkness flooded down from his outstretched arms like a waterfall of thick black oil.

PETER ATKINS

The darkness swept outwards, descending with terrifying swiftness over Taylor.

As his arms spread, Jimmy's coat had flown open. Where his belly should have been was a dark mirror in which Taylor could conveniently watch his own reflection as it screamed.

12

"I'm not sure she can hear us," Shelley said.

She was trying, by the example of her calm tone, to teach some of the kids a little lesson in patience. But Royston Beddowes wasn't having any of it.

"Let us in!" he shouted again, his seven-year-old voice angry and demanding. "Let us in!"

He rapped his knuckles for what seemed like the eighty-seventh time on the red plastic of the playhouse door and Shelley began to feel a sneaking and shameful sympathy for the cherished belief of those unenlightened Victorians who held that children should be seen and not heard.

She didn't know if she was pissed off more by Royston's entitled impatience or by the passive-aggressive silence of Audrey, the little girl who was occupying the newly completed playhouse and was holding the door shut against Royston and the three other kids who were equally eager to get inside.

"Seriously, Royston," Shelley said, holding on to her kind voice by a fraying thread, "perhaps Audrey can't hear you." She knew very well that of course Audrey could hear him—half the fucking campus could probably hear him—but she thought she knew the game that Audrey wanted to play. "Look," she said, pointing to the plastic telephone that Audrey had passed out of the playhouse's window almost as soon as she'd gotten inside and which was now sitting on the floor ignored by all four of the kids. "Perhaps—"

"I don't care!" Royston yelled. And then added "I don't care!" in case his position on the matter required some clarification.

"Second amendment doesn't seem like such a bad idea now, does it?" said Molly, breezing past Shelley on her way to the rear of the room. Not, you know, stopping to help or anything. Just smirkingly grateful for the passing amusement. Real nice.

Shelley reached over and dragged the toy phone across the floor until it was nearer to her. She raised the plastic handset, put it to her face, and jabbed at the buttons on the base unit to make its little internal bell ring. Royston, thank Christ, was catching his breath between shouts.

"Hello, Audrey?" Shelley said into the phone. "Can you hear me? This is Ms. Campbell. Audrey, your friends are here and they want to come visit with you."

"We're not *visiting!*" shouted Royston. "It's not *her* house! It's *our* house!"

Great. Now he was Karl fucking Marx.

The other three were gazing at Royston with open admiration but fortunately, before they could start looking around for any handy pitchforks with which to storm Audrey's plastic Winter Palace, the red door opened from the inside.

"Hello, everybody!" said Audrey, plainly delighted by the unexpected company. She was about halfway into her hostess's smile of welcome when her eyes went wide and her little body jumped in sudden shock.

Shelley nearly jumped too.

Taylor Smith was screaming.

Shelley spun her head around to the rear of the room, to see Taylor jerking his head up from where it had been lying on his folded arms on the desk at which he was sitting. He must have started screaming in his sleep and was still too confused by his sudden waking to stop.

Molly was already on it—halfway to his desk, her comforting arms reaching out in readiness.

"Taylor?" she said. "It's okay, sweetheart. It's okay."

Shelley, unconsciously reaching out herself to stroke reassuringly at the shoulders and heads of the startled kids beside her, could see that Taylor was far from sure that it was okay, whatever Ms. Edwards might think. Still barely out of the grip of whatever daytime dream had troubled him, he was twitching in his chair as if some asshole had wired it up to an electrical outlet, and his eyes were flicking crazily around the room as if fearing attack from any corner at any moment.

Molly got nearer to him but was wise enough to stop when, still screaming, he put his arms out protectively to ward her off.

"Molly, he's not back yet!" Shelley called to her, trying to keep urgency or alarm out of her voice for the sake of the other kids and not doing a great job of it.

For three endless awful seconds, Taylor continued to scream.

"Taylor!" Molly snapped, her voice hard and demanding.

Shelley flinched. But, miraculously, Molly's instinct proved correct. The boy stopped screaming, his eyes focused on Molly, and—absurdly, touchingly, mercifully—suddenly the only expression on his face was a completely normal one: mortifying embarrassment.

"What?" he said to Molly, in an almost cute attempt at pretending he didn't know what on earth Ms. Edwards was making such a fuss about.

Royston and Audrey and one or two of the others giggled, and the moment was over. The other kids started scrambling inside the playhouse. Shelley watched them for a second to be sure there were no more territorial wars about to break out and then looked back over at Taylor and Molly.

Molly had her arms around him now and Taylor was smart and grateful enough not to pretend he wasn't happy about it.

Shelley had a brief moment to feel relieved, and then Taylor shifted in the comfort of Molly's embrace and looked back across the room towards Shelley.

He looked at the plastic phone in her hand. He looked at the playhouse. He looked at Shelley.

The look in his eyes made her feel awful. It was fearful and accusing.

"Taylor…?" she said, and her voice was cautious and apologetic, though she had no idea what for.

Taylor didn't reply.

*

The bus that dropped the kids off and picked them up was a legit School Bus. It was another normalizing element for them, one that Molly had insisted upon and organized. It was a normalizing element for Shelley too, come to that, and it was almost always a pleasure when she and Molly would walk the kids across the campus at the end of the period and watch them climb on board the bus and, sometimes, depending on how they were feeling, wave goodbye through its windows to the women they thought of as their teachers.

Today was different, of course.

It was probably true that, at some of the other windows,

some of the other kids were waving and smiling as the bus began to pull away onto the city streets. But Shelley was only looking at one window, the one where Taylor was sitting. He was turned in his seat to look out the window but he was neither smiling nor waving. He was just staring at her. The specific expression of wary accusation that he'd worn in the classroom had gone, which was something, but it had been replaced by a close relative of the alarmingly blank stare that he wore in his strange quiet spells when he'd stare out at the world. He wasn't looking at the world in general this time, though. He was looking directly at Shelley, his gaze fixed and unwavering.

She was doing her best, of course. She wasn't avoiding his eyes. She was even attempting a friendly smile, to try to let him know that everything was okay between them, that things hadn't changed.

But his expression didn't alter at all until he was lost to her sight as the bus merged into the early afternoon traffic.

Molly'd been cool, not saying anything until Shelley could be done with her brave face. Now she turned to her.

"Day's over," she said. "Switch it off."

Shelley shook her head, more in regret than denial. "It's not that easy," she said.

"Well, it needs to be," Molly said, tapping Shelley's elbow gently to start them both walking back across the campus toward the staff and faculty lot where their cars were parked.

"Seriously," Molly continued. "If I got bent out of shape every time one of the little bastards got mad at me, I'd—"

"No," Shelley said, cutting her off. "That's not it. He wasn't mad. He seemed...afraid of me. That's what's freaking me out."

"Taylor's a troubled kid, Shelley."

"But I'm supposed to be part of the solution, not part of the problem."

Molly looked at her. "Well, we can trade em-oh-dubya cliché lines for as long as you like, but I'm really not sure it's going to help."

Shelley didn't know what MOW meant, and knitted her eyebrows at Molly.

"Really?" Molly said. "You're really that young? I'm really that out of touch?"

"For shizzle, my Mizzle," Shelley said. And then—'cause God forbid Molly actually picked up on it and made a frickin' idiot out of herself by trying it out on younger members of her family: "Such usage strictly ironic these days, by the way."

Molly half-grinned. "That's better," she said, and Shelley realized that she'd stepped out of her worries about Taylor and herself long enough to have made a joke. Not, like, a good one or anything but still. They'd reached their cars now and were standing by them.

Molly looked at her appraisingly. "Better," she repeated, "but not enough. You can't keep taking this crap home with you. I believe the time has finally come to introduce you to Molly Edwards' Cure for All Work-induced Worries."

She opened the passenger door of her car and nodded at Shelley. "Get in," she said. And then, off Shelley's puzzled look: "Get in! I'll bring you back. Ain't going that far."

What the hell, Shelley got in. She watched as Molly got in the driver's side, but she gave her friend a dubious look while she strapped herself in the seatbelt. "This 'cure'," she said, "does it involve copious amounts of alcohol and foreign sailors?"

Moontown

"You wish," said Molly. And then, almost as an afterthought, "Fleet Week's in March, not October. Did your mother teach you *nothing?*"

Molly's car pulled out into traffic. With intent. Like traffic better pay some fucking attention.

*

"You've got to be kidding me," Shelley said.

That made three times she'd said it since Molly'd parked her car outside the strip-mall video arcade and led Shelley inside. But Molly had yet to confirm that she was kidding, and Ashton Kutcher and his camera squad had yet to show up to tell Shelley that dude, she was being *Punk'd*.

On the massively big video screen directly ahead of Shelley, at least fifteen shaven-headed and heavily-armed muscular thugs darted and weaved for cover in the usual generic urban wasteland setting, each of them blasting their weapons directly out of the screen at the viewer.

A floating gun-sight was sweeping across the picture, taking its calm and professional time in the face of the enemy fire. Suddenly though, two rocket-propelled grenades blasted forward and took out two of the thugs. As they exploded in a computer-graphic death of blood and viscera, Molly finally broke her silence.

"Meet God, motherfuckers!" she yelled in delight.

Molly, seated at the arcade game like a woman at ease in her natural environment, was sweeping her console-mounted multi-weapon back and forth and firing ceaseless — and astonishingly accurate — cyber-death at her virtual enemies.

Bam! She took another thug's head clean off his shoulders and whooped in glee. "Too ugly to live," she told his spastically twitching corpse, "too dumb to die!"

Shelley, standing beside and a little behind her, watched in embarrassingly wide-eyed amazement as her friend, this smart and educated forty-five-year-old woman, followed up the semi-kill with a decisive and chest-shattering second shot, and did it as enthusiastically as any pimple-faced fourteen-year-old boy.

The arcade was packed with similar machines. The air was full of the sounds of explosions, crashes, mass slaughter, and the roars of pleasure of the players, most of whom—though astonishingly far from all—were indeed pimple-faced fourteen-year-old boys.

Molly's screen suddenly froze mid-carnage and a message appeared on it: *Accessing Level Three.*

Molly, swinging around briefly in her seat, pulled a five-dollar bill from a pocket and pressed it into Shelley's hand.

"Here," she said. "Go kill something."

Before Shelley could answer, Molly had swung back to her screen, grabbing up her weapon again as a whole new killing-ground opened up for her.

"That's right, asswipes!" she shouted at the screen in what Shelley would swear on a stack of Krafft-Ebings was an almost eroticized excitement. "Come to Mama!"

Bam! Bam! Eyes agleam, Molly returned to the job of crushing her enemies. Shelley was pretty sure that her friend would be just as into hearing the lamentations of their women, had the game thought to provide that Cimmerian option.

Figuring she'd be invisible to Molly until the kill-count reached whatever absurd number was necessary to access

MOONTOWN

level four, Shelley left her to it and moved off down the central aisle of the arcade.

She had Molly's five dollars in her hand and, though she was far from sure she was actually going to use it, she felt it'd be rude not to at least check out the scenarios on the big screens of the endless machines.

At first, nothing caught her eye enough to hold it—each screen seemed to offer nothing more than its own customized variation on the same essential theme: *Keep them coming. Kill them all*—and in the end it was not her eye but her ear that, amidst the rattles of gunfire and roars of explosions, finally picked out something marginally different.

From one of the machines that she'd just passed by without really looking at it, she heard the sounds of a racing engine and the howl of tortured wheels.

Shelley turned back to look at it. The game's flashing logo said *Night Ride*, and its screen was running through a demo:

A point-of-view car—wheel, dashboard, windshield—was hurtling down a dark country road, swerving around absurdly tight hairpin bends and avoiding various obstacles.

Or sometimes not avoiding them.

As Shelley watched, the car on the *Night Ride* screen suddenly veered dangerously up a dark embankment, juddering over its rough grass but somehow managing to turn itself enough to hurtle back down onto the road—where its headlights caught sudden sight of a coyote frozen mid-crossing.

As the car slammed unavoidably into the beast, Shelley felt her body jerk in shock as if feeling the impact.

She stared at the screen, her eyes widening and dismay creeping into her heart.

She hadn't needed to touch anything.

The memory was coming, and coming fast. Overwhelming and complete.

*

Shelley wasn't even sure that Jen liked rap-metal, but that's what she'd found on Shelley's car radio and that's what she'd cranked loud. Real loud.

And this was Jen's night, so whatever floated her boat or, you know, bobbed her barnacles.

The music pounded, the car speakers did their best not to rattle, and Shelley drove through the darkness. She'd been a 'burbs or inner-city girl all her life and real country roads, with their absence of any lights at all and their traffic-free nature late at night, still weirded her out a little.

The occasional flashes of barely glimpsed trees through her windows were her only real clue that she was probably not obeying the posted speed limits. On the other hand, she hadn't seen *a posted speed limit for at least twenty miles, so what the hell. And, come on, what lonely country road traffic cop in his right mind would actually give a speeding ticket to two such hot little numbers as her and Jen?*

In the passenger seat, Jen had her arms raised above her head and through the moon-roof, seat-dancing to the music.

"Whoo! Gonna have some fun tonight!" Jen shouted to the world in general and turned to grin at Shelley.

Shelley grinned back, and gunned the engine a little more. Which wasn't smart, but Jen wanted to feel *things tonight and Shelley was here to help.*

The two-lane blacktop wound narrowly through the dark night like a switchback trail. The landscape was hilly, as far as Shelley could tell, and there were grass verges on each side of the road that climbed steeply upward. Though her car was negotiating each bend successfully, Shelley knew that it wasn't exactly choosing a lane when it did.

Jen, upper body still swaying to the music, had lowered her arms from the open moon-roof and was digging through her purse.

"What do you need?" Shelley said. Shouted, really. Had to, music was so damn loud.

In answer, Jen pulled out a photograph from her purse and flourished it for Shelley to see.

Funny just how much prior knowledge brings to your judgment of a picture, Shelley thought. Because, to anyone without prior knowledge of the prick in question, the picture would be simply a photo of a very handsome young man. To Shelley, though, it was a picture of The Cheating Bastard Who Broke Jen's Heart (Twice).

Shelley looked up from the picture to her friend and pulled an appalled face. "You kept his picture?!*" she said.*

"Only for this," Jen said and, taking out a cigarette lighter, she set fire to the photograph.

"Alright!" Shelley shouted, and banged applause on her wheel with the side of a closed fist.

Jen kept a grip of the picture until the flame really got a hold of it, then raised it up through the moon-roof and let the night winds take it, sending it jetting away behind them, still burning.

Their cheers echoed after it, Jen swiveling in her seat to watch it go and Shelley doing her best to keep it in sight in her rearview as she sped the car on, swerving it around another hairpin bend.

As she straightened the car up on the other side of the curve, its headlights picked out something on the side of the road a few hundred yards ahead. It was neither a tree nor a grassy verge.

"Seriously?" said Shelley, loudly enough for Jen to swing back around in her seat and take a look ahead through the windshield.

The figure on the side of the road was a hitchhiker, a guy as much as this distance would let them tell, waving his outstretched thumb as Shelley's car sped towards him.

"On this road?!" Jen said, as incredulous as Shelley.

Shelley and Jen shared a no-fucking-way look at each other and then shouted in unison:

"Axe-Murderer!!"

They laughed hysterically. The car neared the hitcher.

Shelley—with the active collaboration of the three mojitos inside her from earlier that night—shouted a suggestion to Jen. "Flash him!" she said.

Watching Jen clamber up in her seat, so that her upper body was out of the moon-roof, Shelley swept her car past the hitcher with a threatening curve that made him jump back from the side of the road.

Jen had some threatening curves of her own. Lifting her tank-top to shoulder-height, she exposed her breasts as easily and thoughtlessly as if a *Girls Gone Wild* crew was throwing around money and Tequila shots.

"Read 'em and weep!" she shouted back at the hitcher and then, laughing, climbed back down inside the car.

"The look on his face!" Jen said, making it sound so good that Shelley just had to try to see it. Even though the car was heading into another curve, she looked back over her shoulder. But the hitcher was already vanishing into the distance behind them, whatever expression he wore unreadable to her. Maybe next time. Maybe she'd—

"SHELLEY!!!"

There was real terror in Jen's scream.

Shelley jerked her head forward, looking through the windshield to see the road ahead and the SUV hurtling toward them.

Shelley swerved her car desperately to the right to avoid the collision, praying that the SUV's driver would be smart enough not to move too.

Moontown

And, thank Christ, he was.

And the cars missed each other. Narrowly. But good enough for rock and roll.

And for nearly a whole half-second, Shelley felt good, not even caring about the angry horn of the SUV echoing in the darkness.

Then she realized that she couldn't pull the car out of the emergency swerve and that it was banking up the high grassy verge. Banking steeply. Too steeply. Too fast.

And then it wasn't banking at all. It was cartwheeling through the air and landing upside-down on the blacktop with a sickening crunch.

And suddenly a male voice was saying, "You want this or not?"

Which wasn't right at all.

*

All the other noises came back too, all the noises of the arcade, and Shelley's eyes jerked open.

For a second, she was still disoriented, not sure where she was. All she knew was that a tough and mean looking guy—probably no more than eighteen but almost linebacker-solid—was standing right in front of her, his expression just two degrees shy of overt aggression.

"You want this or *not*?!" he said again.

Shelley finally saw that he was gesturing at the *Night Ride* machine, to which, she realized, she was blocking his access. She shook her head, still confused and shaken by the intense memory visitation, and started to back away.

"No," she said. "No, I'm sorry. I—"

"Yeah, whatever," he said. "Blow me, bitch."

He'd already turned his back on her and was squeezing himself into the *Night Ride* chair.

Shelley was almost as surprised as him when a hand suddenly palm-swiped him across the back of his faux-hawk head.

"What the *fuck*?!" he said, swinging around in the chair, face creased in fury, to see Molly, her hand still raised from slapping him.

Oh shit. Shelley opened her mouth to try to defuse the situation and save her well-meaning friend from a no-gender-bias beating, but she hadn't even got a single placatory word out before Molly's other hand was palm-out at her in a silencing gesture.

Molly wasn't looking at her though. Her eyes were fixed firmly on the guy in the seat. "She's with *me*, crater-face," Molly said. "A little respect."

The guy's mouth opened, ready to hurl invective, and his strong young body flexed, ready to back it up.

But Molly got in first.

"Hey!" she said, her tone cold, hard, and informative. "I'm Molly Fucking Edwards, pencil-dick."

Shelley couldn't believe what happened next. It was like a freaking movie. Murmurs and whispers flew through the air from every gamer within earshot, as if they were extras cued by an assistant director to express profound awe. *"Molly Edwards,"* they said. *"The Mollifier."* That must be her screen-name, Shelley figured, and could only guess at how many high-score lists on how many machines that name must top in order to have produced this reaction.

The guy on the *Night Ride* chair didn't say anything. His face softened into cowed respect.

Molly wasn't quite done with him. "Wanna throw down with me?" she said. "Right now? Name the game, motherfucker. *Galaxon*? *Alley Rumble*? *Livewire*? 'Cause I'll kick your acne-riddled white ass any time you're ready, son."

The guy shook his head. "I'm sorry," he said.

"It's not me you owe an apology to," Molly told him, her tone strategically a little gentler.

The guy turned to face Shelley. "I apologize, ma'am," he said politely, like Molly had just let out his inner nineteen-fifties nice boy, like as soon as he was finished here he'd be right back on his three-speed Schwinn delivering newspapers to Ward and June Cleaver and their neighbors.

Shelley nodded a still-can't-believe-it acknowledgment as Molly took her arm and led her out of the arcade.

Once they were outside in the late afternoon air of the strip-mall, Molly took a moment to sigh with pleasure. "That's what I love about child psychology," she said. "The practical applications."

"*Ma'am*?" said Shelley finally, giving her a look.

Molly arched an eyebrow right back at her. "You prefer *bitch*?" she said, and led her to the car.

13

Shelley shifted aside the two mini-magnets that held Jen's photograph on the fridge door—she'd picked one of Johnny Depp because Jen had dug him and one of the young and feisty Barbara Stanwyck because she figured Jen might have grown to dig her—and handed the picture to Molly.

She'd talked to Molly a little on the way back to the campus and her own parked car, talked enough to make Molly invite herself to follow Shelley back to her apartment to talk some more.

While Molly held the picture and looked at it, Shelley went back to the coffee maker just in time for its brewed-and-ready *beep*. She pulled a couple of mugs from the overhead cabinet.

"Pretty girl," Molly said.

Shelley nodded without looking up from pouring the coffee into their mugs. "Pretty. Smart. Talented," she said. "Going to be an illustrator. Children's books, maybe. Probably going to be a wife and mother too, someday. But none of that's going to happen now. Cream?"

"Black," said Molly.

"Sugar?"

"Two. Listen, it's a terrible thing, what happened." Molly waited till Shelley finally looked up at her. "But nothing you do—or feel—can change it."

"Right," said Shelley. "I should just get over it." She tried to keep the heard-all-that-shit-before out of her voice but didn't do a great job of it.

MOONTOWN

Molly put Jen's photo carefully back in its place before saying anything more. "Well, should you *not* get over it?" she said. "It's been two years, sweetheart."

"Here," Shelley said, handing Molly her coffee. She leaned back against her counter and sipped at her own mug. "You know what people don't understand? It's not that she *died*. It's so much more selfish than that. It's that I couldn't *help* her. I felt so useless, so powerless. I crawled out of that wreck with hardly a scratch but..."

"...you couldn't get her out."

"I tried," Shelley said, "but I couldn't." Shelley felt her eyes filling with tears. She blinked them back. "All I could do was...was listen to her die."

"Oh God..." said Molly.

Shelley heard the horrified empathy in her friend's voice and almost regretted making her feel it, at whatever remove. "I swore that it would never happen again," she said. "That nobody'd ever die on my watch. But Anthony died."

"Shelley—" Molly started to say, but Shelley cut her off.

"And Taylor, today," she said. "Did you see how he *looked* at me? Did you? Like he couldn't trust me. Like I was never going to pull him out, like..."

"Stop!" Molly said. "Listen. Listen to me. You're going to help people. You *are* helping people. Even Taylor. And this whole project of yours, it's potentially groundbreaking. If your weird little friend Alex Drayton wasn't such a control-freak credit-hog maybe you'd realize how fucking important you are."

Shelley waved a hand half-dismissively. "I'm not saying I—"

But Molly wasn't going to let her blank it. "No," she said. "*Hear* that. Please, Shelley. You're going to *save lives*."

Shelley did her best to simply return Molly's stare, to give her nothing else in response. But Molly was just as patient and just as stubborn as she and finally, almost unconsciously, Shelley felt herself give a single acknowledging nod—reluctant and resentful, perhaps, but grateful too.

"Good," said Molly, draining her coffee and putting the mug back down on Shelley's kitchen counter. "And now I gotta go."

Shelley gave another nod, this one easier and friendlier, and neither she nor Molly seemed to feel the need to say anything more until they'd crossed Shelley's living room and were approaching the apartment door.

"Thank you, Molly," Shelley said then. "For that, and for the arcade too."

"Right," said Molly, back in her everyday tell-it-like-it-is mode. "That part was a *big* hit."

Shelley laughed as she opened the apartment door. She watched Molly step out and wondered why her friend stopped mid-step to lean down and look at something that was presumably on the hallway floor beyond the doorway.

"Aha," Molly said. "An admirer?"

She bent down more fully and, when she stood and turned back to Shelley, she was grinning with pleasure and holding a large bouquet of flowers.

"Here," she said, handing it to Shelley and peering inside the gathered flowers. "It doesn't look like there's a card. Must be a *secret* admirer. The best kind."

Shelley could say nothing. She was staring at the bouquet, and feeling already the stirrings of confusion and alarm.

The flowers, luxuriant but fragile, were wild blossoms, absolutely identical to the flowers she had seen in Margaret's recovered memory.

Moontown

*

He was back behind his old friend the cypress tree on the moonlit street outside Shelley's building, sheltered and safe and able to see.

The light in her second-floor living room was still on, and he thought he saw a shadowed movement behind the closed curtains, as if she were watching through a chink to see that her colleague reached her car safely.

She had nothing to worry about. He watched as the woman—her name, he knew, was Molly Edwards—exited the front door of the building and walked toward her vehicle, parked within half a block of Shelley's building. Pretty good for this part of town.

Interesting. A few yards from her car, the Edwards woman paused, turned around, and looked up and down the street as if she could sense she was being watched. The Force was strong in this one.

He tightened up his position behind the cypress, though he didn't really feel it necessary. She was fishing, not targeting, he was sure, and there was a street light between her and him that would render him at most a misshapen shadow.

Nevertheless, he was relieved to watch her shrug the feeling off, get in her car, start it up, and drive away. He guessed she'd probably take a glance in the rearview for something more than oncoming traffic, though, so he remained quite still for a moment or two longer.

Only when her car had turned the corner did Tom Lawson take out his BlackBerry and note the time and duration of her visit.

14

Taylor seemed much better the next time.

He hadn't exactly greeted Shelley with a pat on the ass and a *whassup* but neither had he fixed her with that thousand-yard stare of his or kept a conscious and careful distance from her.

He was even near the playhouse today, which was also progress of a sort, she figured. Not, like, *inside* it or anything—but at least perched in front of its window with two or three other kids having what almost looked like an untroubled conversation.

Shelley was some distance across the room, trying not to look at Taylor too often but checking periodically that Molly—at her desk, catching up on some paperwork—was also keeping a watchful eye on him and the others.

Shelley had her own little group gathered around her whom she was encouraging—or attempting to jump-start—into some craft activities. Plastic scissors, craft paper, and crayons were scattered on the floor in front of the kids but had yet to inspire in them the kind of enthusiasm Shelley had been hoping for. Audrey, who was among them, was half-heartedly playing a kind of miniature hopscotch by skipping her fingers idly through the handle-hoops of one of the pairs of plastic scissors, but that was as good as it had got so far.

"Well," Shelley said to them as brightly as she could, "why don't we start by thinking of things that we like?" Jeez. Big hand for Julie Andrews, ladies and gentlemen, let's hear it for raindrops on roses and whiskers on kittens.

The kids looked up at her, some blankly, some with expressions of puzzled concern. Alright, time to pick a point-person.

"Cameron," she said, "why don't you tell us something that *you* like."

Cameron was a trooper, she'd give him that. And a demonstrative one—his little brow puckered in concentration to let her know that he was giving the matter some serious thought. He took a moment, quite a long moment actually, but Shelley was cool with that. She let him take the time, pleased that he was at least trying, and she was rewarded after a few more seconds by the sight of Cameron's face relaxing into a surprised—and adorable—smile. He had something.

"Mm-hm?" Shelley offered encouragingly.

"Poo," said Cameron. "I like poo."

Audrey gasped and the other kids in the group giggled. Shelley started to shake her head, but she checked herself. Cameron hadn't been consciously going for the laugh, she believed. He'd actually given her an honest response. "No," she said, "that's okay. I guess. Could you draw us some?"

Cameron stared at her for a moment like he couldn't believe his luck and then, nodding enthusiastically, he snatched up a brown crayon and began drawing.

Shelley looked over at She-Who-Hears-Everything and caught her eye to check for approval. Molly, who was still at her desk and now appeared to be involved in a craft project of her own involving real scissors, string, and brown paper, looked up long enough to give Shelley a long-as-he's-happy shrug and continued working on wrapping her parcel.

Inspired by Cameron's example, three of the other kids started grabbing at the paper and the plastic scissors. Shelley watched them set to work and then took another look over to Taylor and the kids outside the playhouse.

They were still sitting, still conversing, but something had changed in their body language and volume level. They were hunkered down, leaning their heads in close to each other, and talking in low whispers. There was something that seemed almost... what?... *conspiratorial* about it, and Shelley felt a curiously disproportionate rush of anxiety wash through her.

"Ms. Campbell?" said a voice behind her.

Shelley turned back to her group to see that Audrey was standing right beside her. She was holding something behind her back, something she obviously didn't want Shelley to see yet.

"Yes, Audrey?" she said.

"Do you have a pin?"

"A pin?" said Shelley. "Well, I'm sure we can get one from Ms. Edwards, sweetheart. Why?"

"I made you a brooch," Audrey said, and brought out from behind her back a hand-colored flower that she had assiduously, albeit approximately, cut out from a piece of craft paper.

"Audrey, that's so nice!" Shelley said, touched as well as pleased. "Thank you very much. Come on; let's go get ourselves a pin."

She stood up and took Audrey by the hand. Before starting across the room to Molly's desk, she looked down at Cameron and the others. "Keep working," she said to them all. "We'll just be a minute."

Moontown

Molly's desk was on the other side of the playhouse, and as Shelley led Audrey past the second group of kids, still crouched towards each other in a semi-huddle and muttering busily and secretly among themselves, she couldn't help but hear a ghostly snatch or two from their whispered exchanges.

"*...when he was scratching at my window...*"

Wait. Was that *really* what Mandy Aronson had just said? Shelley couldn't be completely sure, given how quietly all of them were talking, but there was no doubt about the clarity of Taylor Smith's reply—mainly because he raised his voice to deliver it, raised it just enough to convey the kind of weary contempt for the ill-informed that was depressing to hear in anybody, let alone one so young .

"*His name isn't* Johnny, *it's* Jimmy" he whispered.

Shelley actually felt her brow furrow. Involuntarily. Like her body was moving straight to an expression of puzzled concern without waiting for her slowpoke mind to decide whether there were any grounds for it. She might have let them fight it out, might have let her body take a moment to make its argument, had Audrey not been dragging so eagerly on her hand to get them over to Molly. And, seriously, what had the kid said? Johnny. Jimmy. Jimmy meant nothing to her and Johnny was hardly an unusual name. Could've been talking about his favorite Teen Titan or Power Ranger for all Shelley knew. She let Audrey pull her away.

Molly looked up from her desk as they arrived, and Audrey proudly held up the paper flower for Ms. Edwards to see.

"We need a pin," Audrey said.

"It's a brooch," Shelley added quickly, just in case Molly was about to ask out loud whether the purpose of the pin was to put the raggedy-ass paper out of its fucking misery.

"Oh," said Molly, "a brooch." Not a trace of archness. Shelley was proud of her. "Then we certainly do need a pin."

She produced one from a drawer in her desk and handed it to Shelley, over Audrey's reaching fingers. "Let Ms. Campbell help, honey," she said.

Shelley knelt down in front of Audrey and, making sure the sharp end was always pointing her way, helped the little girl use the pin to attach the flower to her blouse.

Molly watched with approval. "You know what, Audrey?" she said. "That is just lovely. It was very thoughtful of you."

Audrey beamed briefly at Molly and then leaned in close to the still-kneeling Shelley to whisper in her ear.

"He told me that you like flowers," she said.

Shelley's smile vanished in an instant and, without thinking, she grabbed Audrey by the wrist and stared intensely at her. "*Who* told you?" she snapped. "What are you talking about?"

It was almost like she didn't see how startled and scared the little girl looked. Almost like she didn't feel how Audrey tried to pull her frightened hand out of Shelley's tightening grasp, shaking her tiny head in confusion and distress.

"Shelley!" Molly said sharply, up and out from behind her desk and standing over them. "Stop it! Right now."

The raised voice of her friend helped Shelley snap out of it. What the hell was she doing? What the hell was she thinking? She let Audrey go immediately and watched in dismay as the little girl ran back across the room to Cameron and the others, casting a single hurt and accusatory look back over her shoulder at Shelley.

Shelley stood up and turned to face Molly. "Oh my God," she said. "I'm so sorry."

Moontown

Molly held her gaze for a moment—with a look in her eyes that Shelley had never seen before and hoped to never see again—and then looked past her to Cameron's group of kids where Audrey was already sitting and playing with the craft materials again. When she looked back to Shelley, who'd felt unable to say anything that wouldn't have sounded stupid and self-serving, her eyes were gentler.

"Goes without saying that that should *never* happen again," she said, and let Shelley feel it for a good long second. "But she'll be okay. Like I've said before, they're never quite as fragile as we think. Don't beat yourself up too—"

Shelley didn't understand why Molly had broken off speaking, didn't understand why she was looking down at her desk and scanning the various wrapping materials she'd been using moments before. When she spoke again, her voice was quiet and puzzled.

"Where are my scissors?" she said.

Shelley didn't need to wait to see the alarm come into Molly's face. She was feeling it plenty herself. Both of them spun around instantly to stare across the room and Shelley didn't know which felt worse, seeing what she saw or not being surprised by it.

Taylor Smith, with no apparent hurry but with an undeniable quiet and steady purpose, was walking toward Cameron's group. In his hand were the scissors from Molly's desk. Real scissors. Adult scissors. Big, pointed, and sharp.

Shelley tried to think that maybe Taylor just wanted to join in the cut-out activities over there and knew that all the plastic scissors were taken. Or maybe—please God let it just be her imagination—he was making a beeline for Audrey.

Audrey appeared to be leaning toward the second option.

She was staring at Taylor as the pace of his approach increased, her little eyes widening in incipient fear.

Taylor's back was to Shelley and Molly, so Shelley couldn't see whatever expression was on his face. But she had a pretty good idea that it would be blank and terrible. She was already hurtling across the room toward him, her arms outstretched, when Molly's cry—

"Taylor!"

—made the boy swing around in shock, his arms arcing out unconsciously and the sharp point of the closed scissors slashing right across Shelley's reaching palm.

As she cried out in pain, blood flying from her wounded hand, Taylor dropped the scissors immediately, any blank expression that might have been on his face wiped away and replaced by a genuinely horrified look at what he had done to her.

"I'm sorry!" he shouted. "I'm sorry!"

Shelley crouched down at once and gathered him to her, hugging him tightly with her good arm while holding the bloodied one away.

"Shush, shush," she said. "It's okay, Taylor. It's okay."

She pressed him more completely to her and Taylor, weeping in a mix of relief and confusion, buried his face in her hair.

By the time Molly reached them she already had a roll of bandage in her hand and, without disturbing Shelley's comforting of the distraught boy, she knelt down and started dressing Shelley's hand.

Shelley turned slightly so that she could look at Molly's face. What she mainly saw there, unsurprisingly, was sympathy and concern. Beneath them, though, she knew that Molly was beginning to wonder just exactly what the hell was going on.

Shelley had no answer for Molly's unspoken question. At least not one that she could yet put into words.

15

The streets and the sidewalks were busy, which was absolutely fine with Margaret Paris.

She was among a bunch of pedestrians at a crowded street corner on her usual route home and was waiting, almost as patiently as she imagined everyone else was, for the walk signal.

Margaret felt alright. She knew that the light was going to change. She hadn't even needed to start her private calming exercise of telling herself that the light would change in a certain number of seconds and then counting them off (the trick of course being to purposely pick a too-high number in order to prompt the placebo relief of not actually reaching it before the light in fact changed—or the door in fact opened or the elevator in fact moved or whatever out-of-her-control thing in fact did whatever she needed it to do in order to make her feel safer).

And the light indeed changed, and the people started crossing the intersection, and Margaret, safely among them, made her way to the other side.

Once she was on the opposite sidewalk, she continued walking purposefully along until she reached the next corner. No light this time, just a simple right turn into the cross street.

There were considerably fewer people on this smaller side street, of course, but Margaret hardly hesitated before starting down it and covering the single block that took her to the next intersection where again she would make a turn. She hardly gave this one any thought because she knew it would put her back on a bigger and busier block and she'd be more than halfway home. She turned the corner…

…and was suddenly facing a vast open space.

Margaret gasped in shock, feeling the panic begin to flood her body, not just at the emptiness of the space but at the terrible unexpectedness of it. She looked around to try to orient herself, to try to see what the hell had just happened.

It was the area where, over the past few days, she'd seen the city work crew arriving and setting up. Now she saw just how much work they'd managed to get done.

Buildings were actually *gone*, leveled into empty stretches of flat earth, and sidewalks had been dug up and demolished or discarded. What had been—only this *morning*—a busy city intersection was now a distressingly large wasteland.

And an all-but deserted one. Though parked trucks and porta-huts dotted the perimeter of the work area, all of them were unattended and unmanned now that the shift had knocked off. But it didn't look like the area had been closed to either traffic or pedestrians. Thin metal rods marked the street corners and long plastic tapes signified the walkways.

Margaret saw that opposite her—on the other side of what used to be the road—there was still a functioning traffic signal. As she gazed in distress at the awful empty openness, which was already—*just your imagination, just your fear, not really happening*—growing wider longer bigger scarier, the walk signal turned green and Margaret seized on it, focusing on the green light as it were a beacon of safety.

She judged the distance and her choices: The street was very wide, always had been, with what used to be a median halfway across it, but once she was over it she'd practically be home. If she hadn't had that breakthrough session with Shelley the other day, she realized, she'd already be turning around and heading—no, let's be honest, *fleeing*—back in the other direction to swallow a pill, wait for it to work, and find a taxi rank.

Biting her lip, summoning her nerve, Margaret started across the intersection, walking briskly and keeping her eyes fixed on the green light.

Ten steps in, she knew she'd made a mistake: the walk was feeling longer than it should; the beckoning green light was seeming to recede rather than to come closer.

Margaret quickened her pace and instinctively, even though both pedestrians and vehicles seemed to be avoiding the work area, she looked up and around to check for traffic, which was another mistake. The openness around her—and she was already, however irrationally, sensing a sentient malice to it—began to expand, its perimeters gleefully receding, its horizon cruelly pulling back, just as it had once done for her younger self, just as it had been waiting all these years for the opportunity to do again.

Margaret heard herself whimper but snapped her eyes away from the now tauntingly distant green light back down to her feet. She forced herself on, pushing her frightened legs one after the other, watching her fearful feet take one step, two steps, three, until she reached the confusion of rods and tape that marked the area where the median had been.

"Halfway there," she said to herself. "Halfway there…"

She took a deep breath, almost daring to let it make her feel a little better, and looked back up and across at the light. Which, as if waiting for her to see it do so, chose that precise moment to turn a decisive and awful red.

Moontown

Instinctively, Margaret stopped right where she was, staring in horror at the flashing *Don't walk... Don't walk...* of the signal.

"No," she said. Not to herself, not really, but to whatever teasingly cruel force her terrified mind believed was deliberately doing this to her. "No, please..."

She glanced all around herself in a wild and growing panic and found no reassurance at all. Overhead, the afternoon sun had disappeared behind a solid bank of heavy gray cloud. The light everywhere was now diffused and hazy, and growing more so by the second, like there was a thickening fog sweeping in eagerly from every direction.

"Stop it," she pleaded, knowing that she sounded seven years old again. "Please stop it."

The edges of the world were disappearing. Everything was becoming a single gray mass, oppressive and tailor-made, a void created especially for her.

Margaret snapped her head back to the signal as if, despite its redness of refusal, it was now the only tiny anchor of solidity in a world of foggy nothingness. It wasn't flashing the words anymore. It was just a simple bright red circle, a circle that, even as she looked at it, began to recede back into the gray misty distance.

"No!" Margaret shouted and began to head out desperately toward the vanishing light, realizing almost incidentally that the world was not only vanishing to sight but to sound. All she could hear was the beating of her own racing heart, which was pounding as loudly as if, invisible in the all-encompassing fog, some stray city worker had come back to kick one of the abandoned jackhammers into life.

Ahead of her—*increasingly* ahead of her no matter how

fast she ran—the circle of light began to drain itself of color, the distinct bright red giving way to a dull silver gray as it retreated from her into what now seemed a very far distance.

Margaret blinked, and wiped at her eyes as if somehow by doing that she could clear the surrounding mistiness, but when she looked again the fog was not only thicker than ever but also had the shining moistness of a cloud bank pregnant with rain. Just ahead of her, for one or two impossible seconds, the sheen of that moisture suddenly shimmered into a solid bank of reflective liquid, like something that was half mirage and half mirror hovering briefly and magically in the dense swirling fog. And in that briefly formed looking glass Margaret saw a perfect reflection of herself, a reflection of herself as a terrified child whose anguished movements and frightened face mirrored those of her adult self perfectly.

As Margaret screamed, the rain mirror vanished back into foggy moistness and she could see again, in the distance, the silver gray orb that she'd once foolishly dreamed was a streetlight.

It was bigger now and had settled on the crest of the horizon.

There was little doubt left in Margaret's mind about what it was.

It was the moon. The rising moon.

Dark shadows flittered across its silver surface like raging channels of pitch-black water, coalescing into a huge central mass of a vaguely humanoid shape, just as Margaret had seen them do once long ago.

"Oh God," she whimpered. "Please no…"

And Mister Moonlight stepped off the moon and into the

Moontown

gray featureless void in front of Margaret, as if any ridiculous notion of the rules of perspective were for much lesser beings than he.

Margaret fell to her knees, trembling in fear, as the shadowed form of Mister Moonlight swept toward her, carrying enveloping darkness in its wake like viscous trails from where it had peeled itself clear of its shell within the moon.

Margaret raised her sobbing head to look at him, just as the darkness washed over her terrified face.

"Hello, Margaret," said Mister Moonlight. "I'm back…"

As she felt herself swallowed by the darkness, Margaret heard her own scream cut off, heard instead as if from far away an urgent and deafening raspy blare…

*

The few pedestrians near the road works heard the desperate blasting of the horn, and most of them looked over in time to see the accident happen.

The truck, plainly doing its best to brake but just not having time or distance on its side, slammed into the elderly woman who was frozen on her knees right in the middle of the intersection.

With a sickening thud of shattering bones, the woman was flung several yards through the air to land heavily on the ground, her dead limbs splayed like a rag doll.

The truck jerked to a halt and the driver leapt out of his cab as some of the witnesses came running over to form a small crowd gathered around what was pretty obviously a corpse.

"Oh!" said a young woman who was wearing some kind of Food Court franchise uniform. "Look at her face!"

The dead woman's features were frozen in a rictus of terror, her lifeless eyes wide open.

"She was kneeling down!" the truck driver said, his voice shaken and defensive. "I didn't see her..."

Most of the murmured comments from the crowd were supportive of him. There was a *You're right, buddy* and a *She was kneeling down*. An overly tanned guy in a business suit said, "She must have been fucking crazy!" and the food court girl gave him a look like whatever the woman had been doing she was dead and he was crossing the line.

"And the light was red," said the driver. "It was red!"

An older man stepped forward from the crowd to take a closer look down at the body. "She couldn't have seen it," he said.

The driver looked up at him quizzically.

The older guy shrugged as if trying to explain what he meant. "Her mind must have been somewhere else," he said.

16

Alex Drayton was a little curious about the bandage on Shelley's left hand. He'd asked her about it but all she'd said was that there'd been an accident in the annex room.

He wondered what had happened, and if it had had anything to do with prompting this surprise nighttime visit of hers. Right now, he had her lying back on his recliner in his darkened private office. Her eyes were closed and he was standing behind her, rubbing gently and rhythmically at her temples. Which of course he was always happy to do, but he was still a trifle puzzled by her sudden need to see him and why she'd accepted this after-hours appointment—which he'd explained was the only way he could make himself available today—rather than wait till tomorrow.

"Tell me again why we're doing this?" he said.

He was somewhat surprised by how drowsy her voice already sounded when she answered him. In fact, answering him at all sounded like an effort for her. She'd only been on her back for two minutes, so he could tell that this was something more than her usual submission to his relaxation techniques. She was actively collaborating, willing herself into sleep as quickly as possible.

"It's...memory," she said, her words almost slurred, as if they were being transmitted from somewhere far away and something was interfering with the signal, "...about memory...I have to..."

"It's alright, Shelley," Alex said soothingly, now that he

saw how near she already was to surrendering to it. "We can talk later. Just drift, don't talk."

"…something we all forget," she murmured, "…but the children…they remember…"

"Shh," said Alex, actually quite excited about how fast she could go under when she really wanted to. "Breathe easy. Let yourself relax. Let yourself go."

Looking over the back of the recliner, he could literally see her relaxing, see her allowing her body to become languorous and limp. It wasn't so much a question of willing it, he knew, more a matter of getting the will out of the way. It was becoming easy for her to do by now, like a learned response that was evolving into instinct.

"Wherever you go, you're safe there," he said, his voice quiet and soft. "You're only watching. Only remembering."

Alex wondered if she'd even heard him. If she had, his voice had probably already seemed to be part of the thoughtscape she was entering rather than the reality she was leaving. Her breathing had become deep and rhythmic, though she was likely as unaware of that as she was that Alex was gently letting his hands slip away from her temples. She was sliding almost effortlessly into sleep, and Alex was pretty sure that she didn't feel it at all when her eyelids began to flicker…

*

…and she didn't, because she was already feeling her hair whip around her face as the night winds buffeted in through the open moon-roof of her car.

She was speeding along the twisting country road, looking up at her

Moontown

rearview to check out the burning photograph of Jen's bastard spiraling away behind them. Jen, half-turned in her seat, was looking back over her shoulder through the rear window so that she too could watch that little piece of her unwanted past disappear into the dark.

Jen shifted in her seat to look at Shelley and smile. Shelley smiled back and gunned the car around the next turn.

*

Alex stood and watched Shelley's eyelids shiver as the eyes beneath them swept back and forth in REM. He was patient and still for quite some time before he moved out from behind the recliner.

When he did move, he moved slowly and he moved quietly. Neither stricture was, truth be told, quite necessary— he knew that Shelley was deeply under by now and unlikely to be woken by the sound of his movements—but he had always preferred to be cautious in these circumstances.

He walked the few paces forward that were needed to put him right beside the reclining girl and then, having checked her face one more time to see that her eyes were still closed and dreaming, he let his own eyes begin a slow and luxurious tour of her body; the swell of her breasts, the flatness of her stomach, the curve of her hips.

He knew that just an inch or so below her navel she had a small mole. He had been privately fond of it ever since first catching an accidentally thrilling glimpse of it some weeks earlier when a T-shirt she was wearing had ridden up over her belly during a careless stretch to pick a book from an upper shelf. He considered for a moment and decided that it would be useful to be able to look at the mole while doing what he was going to do. So he reached out a hand to the lowest button on her blouse and undid it—just one little button, silly girl, nothing to make a fuss about—and spread the blouse slightly apart, no more than necessary, just enough to reveal the mole sitting there teasingly on a naked inch of her lower stomach.

He lifted his hand up again and then brought it to rest, softly but decisively, on the curve of her upper thigh, which was smooth, soft, and excitingly warm beneath his cupping hand.

He was almost ready now. He leaned down and in—still slowly, still carefully—until his face was only inches from Shelley's neck and shoulders.

He breathed in, gently but deeply, savoring her scent.

*

"Hey," Jen said. "How about some music?"

She leaned down to the car radio and began punching some of the pre-sets.

Shelley at first had no idea why she felt troubled by this, and then recognized that it was nothing more than the weird dislocation of déjà vu. She felt not only as if she had been here before but that, when she had been, music had already been playing.

"Didn't we have *music?" she said and then wished she hadn't because the feeling was already fading. In fact, looking out her windshield at the endless stretch of arrow-straight road ahead of her, she wondered —the way you always do with déjà vu once it's gone—how she could have ever thought she'd been here before.*

Jen straightened up from messing with the radio and lounged back in her seat.

MOONTOWN

"Well, it's official," she said. "We're beyond the reach of civilization."

"Huh?" Shelley said. "What do you mean?"

"No radio. Can't get a signal."

"Oh..." Shelley knew she sounded distracted. She was *distracted. Because now she was feeling that the feeling she'd been feeling—*Wow. So sorry Mrs. Kirkham, seventh-grade vocabulary and grammar*—was more to do with the fact that she* should *recognize all that was going on and that certain things were conspiring against her.*

Like that disturbingly straight road, for example.

She stared out at it, feeling her face pucker in concentration as if she could somehow force the recovery of some gnawing alternative memory.

"Probably just as well," said Jen. "The radio might have disturbed the kids."

What?

Shelley's eyes shot up to her rearview.

Sitting bunched together in the back seat of her car were three little children. Shelley felt two things at once, and both felt equally true. She'd never seen these kids before. And their names were Taylor, Cameron, and Audrey.

She jerked in shock and the car swerved dangerously.

"Jesus!" said Jen. "Pick a freaking lane, willya?" Giving Shelley a baby-on-board look, she turned around in her seat to take a look at the kids.

"You guys okay?" she said to them.

She got no answer, and Shelley glanced in the rearview again to see why.

It looked like the kids were way too engrossed in what they were doing to pay attention to some stupid grownup's question. With deep and wordless concentration, they were swapping trading cards back and forth, each of them eagerly fitting individual cards to complete sequences or runs within their own pack. Shelley had never been a sports card collector when she was a little kid, but she certainly remembered the obsessiveness of those of her classmates who had been.

"Guess they're okay," Jen said, as she turned back to Shelley.

Shelley, still looking out the windshield at that straight unending highway, asked her friend a question. She was surprised at how tentative and apologetic her own voice was, like she knew how dumb she sounded but had to ask anyway.

"Where are we?" she said.

Jen didn't answer.

Shelley tried again. "Where are we going?" she said.

She still didn't get an answer. The fuck? Was Jen trying to bond with the kids, to recapture her own childhood by mentally re-sorting her own long lost collection of Laverne & Shirley *trading cards or something?*

"Jen?" Shelley said. "Jen! Can you hear me?"

She looked more carefully at her friend. Jen was sitting very still and was staring straight ahead. It was like she hadn't heard a thing.

But suddenly she replied, her voice very matter-of-fact like there'd been no weird delay at all. "Not really," she said. "Reception's bad out here."

"What?"

"Can't get a signal."

Jen was very still. Strangely still. And somehow paler than before, and there were ghosts of deep black circles under her oddly blank eyes.

"Jen...?" Shelley said, feeling suddenly that she was in the middle of a game where everybody knew the rules except her.

Worse, she felt that even if someone took the time to explain the nature of the game to her it wouldn't make her happy at all. Quite the opposite, in fact.

Jen was still and silent for another long beat and then suddenly spoke again, not to Shelley but to the kids. Her voice was loud and had a

Moontown

stunningly artificial brightness, like somebody had just found the kids a foster mother from Stepford:

"How's it coming back there?!"

Taylor's voice matched Jen's for excitement, but had at least the virtue of sounding genuine. "Full house!!" he said and leaned forward to hand a spread of five cards to Jen.

She took them and then held them up for Shelley to see. "Check it out," she said, like this was the greatest thing ever.

Shelley checked it out. The cards were arced out like a wide-spread poker hand so that she could see all five of them pretty clearly. They were like a cross between old-school baseball cards—in their head-and-shoulders portrait shot framing—and traditional Tarot Cards—in their primary colors within black outlines pictorial style. The portraits each had the name of the—what? player?*—running along the top of the card in bright, kid-friendly, Topps Bubble Gum Company circa 1963 lettering.*

Each portrait appeared essentially to be of the same person, but on each card he—He? Why did she want to say it?*—was wearing a different costume. Wasn't just costumes, though, was it? Shelley felt several words jostling for position in her thoughts, and she wasn't very fond of any of them:*

Personae; avatars; incarnations.

The face was shadowed unsettlingly, as if it were lit chiaroscuro style from a light source that originated somewhere other than the world. It was human-looking but...well, just wrong *somehow...as if she were looking at a human mask that something had pulled over its quite different face for the sheer amusement value of it.*

The names on the cards read like a roll call from some corner of the Inferno where they were really big on snappy nicknames: Mister Moonlight; Johnny in the Dark; The Ragman; Jimmy Midnight; King Shadow.

"He's waiting for his ride," said Jen.

Shelley had been staring at the cards, trying to understand how they made her feel—you know, other than freaked the fuck out—but Jen's words, and the disturbingly flat calmness of their delivery, pulled her eyes back to the road.

Fifty yards ahead, picked out by her car's lights and swathed in a long black coat like something from a spaghetti Western, a hitchhiker was standing with his thumb out.

The hitcher's other hand held a piece of card with his destination written on it. That's *new, Shelley thought, without quite understanding what she meant by it. He was still too far away for her yet to read the sign clearly.*

As Shelley's car closed the distance between them, the hitcher leaned forward eagerly as if not merely hoping but expecting the car to stop.

"He's waiting for his ride," said Jen. Flat and calm, just like she'd said it a moment before. Identical, in fact. Like it wasn't a case of her simply repeating the words, but more like someone had pressed a replay *button on a recording.*

"Well, he can keep right on waiting," Shelley said.

As she swept the car past him, giving a wide berth and not slowing down at all, Shelley looked past Jen out the passenger-side window to get a good look at him.

The hitcher's face—its dark eyes locking unerringly on Shelley's in the second it took to pass him—was the face from the trading cards.

Shelley could see his hand-lettered hitching sign now too, its requested destination plainly visible. It read: Moontown.

Shelley snapped her eyes back straight ahead and gunned the car down the road, leaving him and his sign in the dust.

She risked a glance into her driver-side mirror and was rewarded with the reassuring sight of the hitcher's figure dwindling in the distance she was putting between them.

Shelley looked back out at the road ahead and then, after a moment,

Moontown

turned to see how Jen was doing.
Jen was gone.
The hitcher was sitting in the passenger seat.
Shelley began to scream.

*

Shelley, the scream dying on her lips, flung herself up into a sitting position on the recliner in Alex's office.

Although she knew immediately where she was—knew that she was back in the world, knew that the memory, the dream, the whatever, was over—her body still needed a few seconds to flick the off switch on all the alarm bells that had been triggered within it, and she looked around wildly, wide-eyed and gasping for breath.

At first, she thought she was alone, thought that Alex had actually left her there unattended and vulnerable in her sleep-state. But it wasn't that. Apart from the very soft and dim light of the standing lamp beside the recliner, the office was in complete darkness, and Alex, who must have moved into the chair behind his desk at some stage while she was under, was nothing but a shadowed outline far across the room.

When she initially saw the dark shape behind the desk, Shelley felt a tiny but very precise stab of fear that it might be someone else, but then Alex's voice came out of the shadows.

"Are you okay?" he asked.

Shelley squinted across the room at him. "Is that you?" she said.

"Who else would it be?" he said and then, as if only belatedly registering her tone, "You sound upset, Shelley. Did something... unexpected happen?"

"The memory," she said. "It wasn't real. It wasn't... right."

"What do you mean?"

"The stuff that happened—it isn't what *happened*. It was different this time."

Alex sounded interested. "Different?" he said. "In the sense that you recovered more details, perhaps? That a clearer picture began to emerge?"

"No," said Shelley. "*Different*. Like it wasn't really my memory anymore. Like..." She broke off, unsure how to say how it had felt.

Alex on the other hand seemed happy to venture an opinion. "Like you weren't in charge of what was to be seen?" he said.

"Yeah," she said. "Something like that."

"Well, I think that's good, Shelley," he said. "I think that means that we're getting places."

"The only places I was getting to were places that don't exist," she said.

"Or getting to places you've allowed yourself to forget," he said. "To memories that you've buried."

"Bullshit. The accident was two years ago and I've remembered it—in excruciating detail—every day since."

"Perhaps it's not the accident you need to remember."

"What do you mean?"

"Perhaps it's something else. Other memories starting to break through."

Shelley still couldn't see him properly and she was starting to be bugged by the strange authority that his voice seemed to borrow from the darkness.

"Can we get some lights on in here?" she said.

Alex seemed either to not hear her, or to be too busy still

musing on what she'd said earlier to pay any attention to such a mundane request. "Driving to a place that you've forgotten," he said. "Chosen to forget, perhaps. Hmm. Do you think that—"

Shelley cut him off. "Alex?" she said. "Lights?"

"Let's keep it like this for the moment," he said. His voice was perfectly calm and professionally kind. "I want to pursue this thought. And I don't want to break the mood." He paused a moment. "Okay?"

Shelley wanted to disagree, to insist on what she wanted, but she let it go. He was the doctor. "Okay," she said.

"Good," said Alex, and Shelley swore she could hear a slight satisfied inhalation as if he was savoring her acquiescence.

He continued. "Now let's think about Anthony and Margaret. In both cases, we had to break through one thing to get to the one that counted, didn't we?"

"So you think..." Shelley began, but was interrupted.

"What do *you* think?" he said.

Jeez. Therapist-speak 101. Like she wasn't almost as much a colleague as she was a patient. Why was he being such a dick? "I think I never collected baseball cards when I was a little girl," she said. "Especially not ones featuring a starting line-up from Hell."

From the shadows, Alex sighed. A little theatrically, in Shelley's humble opinion.

"Shelley," he said, "I'm sensing resistance. "I think you should try to approach this with more of an open mind." Again, that pause. Again, that push for verbal surrender. "Okay?"

This time Shelley was silent.

"Shelley?" he said, a tiny tone of stern warning in his voice, like he'd just told a child to do something and was going to be cross if he had to repeat himself.

"Okay," said Shelley.

"You know," he said, like he'd really been giving it some thought, "*okay* is such a... half-hearted word. Could you say *yes?*"

"Look, can we just—"

"Could you say *yes?*"

"Yes!"

"Mmm," he said, and this time his pleasure in her obedience was more overt, more self-satisfied. "Could you say *Yes, sir?*"

"What?!"

"Could you say *Yes, Daddy?*"

What the fuck *was* this? Shelley started to scramble off the Recliner. "Who the hell do you think you're talking to?" she said.

But Alex wasn't really listening to her anymore.

Instead, as Shelley leapt to her feet, letting her fury build, he was slipping into a creepy chant...

"Say *Yes, Daddy.* Say Yes. Say Yes. Yes. Yes."

...which had the quickening obsessive rhythm of some sick masturbatory mantra...

"Yes. Yes! YES!! YES!!!"

...like there was a distinct and revolting possibility that he might actually be jerking off back there in the dark.

Shelley grabbed angrily at the standing lamp beside the recliner and tilted it violently to shine its light back toward Alex's desk...

"YES!!! **YES!!! YES!!!!**"

…and the second the pool of soft light hit him, Alex's voice cut off instantly and completely.

Which was hardly surprising.

Because Alex was dead.

His body was propped up in his chair, his arms hanging uselessly and lifelessly and his head tilted impossibly to one side as if lolling on an utterly broken neck.

Shelley surprised herself by not screaming, but she did take an involuntary step or three backwards until the feel of the recliner against her legs stopped her and she stood, still holding the lamp like a spotlight and staring in uncomprehending horror at Alex Drayton's blood-drained face, at his wide-open lifeless eyes.

One of which suddenly winked at her.

"You'll have to forgive me," said the voice from Alex's mouth. "I appear to have gotten quite carried away there for a moment or two."

There was no doubt that Alex was dead. His body was completely motionless and his face completely frozen. Well, not completely frozen: the jaw, hideously, was opening and closing with the rhythmic simplicity of a poorly operated ventriloquist's dummy, flapping up and down with a vaudevillian looseness that bore no practical relationship to the words emerging impossibly from the corpse's mouth.

"Now," the voice continued. "Where were we?"

Shelley realized that she'd been frozen in a fear-induced paralysis only when it finally snapped. Her body had taken over, turning her around and making her drop the lamp and run, making her fling open the door from the private office and run into the bigger group study room beyond.

The lights were out in there too, but the blinds weren't

drawn and there was enough moonlight coming in from the world outside for Shelley to see the other door, the one at the far end of the room, the door to the corridor, the door that would let her out of this madness, or at least away from her immediate proximity to it. She raced for the door, not wanting to look behind her but unable to resist one quick glance over her shoulder back into the private office.

She wished she hadn't.

Behind its desk, Alex's corpse was twitching—or being twitched—into an obscene parody of life, its limp arms jerking upwards spastically as if some unseen and malicious puppeteer was trying to get it to stand and walk. The light from the standing lamp—still on the floor where Shelley had dropped it—was now hitting the dead thing from a creepily low angle that deepened and dramatized the shadows and the paleness of its awful face like retro footlights in some hellish cabaret.

There was a high-pitched animal keening in the air that Shelley thought for a moment was the latest horror to issue from the thing's mockery of a mouth until she realized it was in fact the atonal melody of her own terror. She told herself to stop, had no fucking idea if she actually did, and kept running across the room trying to think only of the door and the way out.

Once at the door, she grabbed at its handle like it was the single lifebelt thrown on a freezing ocean and flung the door wide, ready to race down the corridor.

But someone was standing in the doorway.

Shelley screamed, as much in shocked surprise as in fear, but a second later saw that the figure blocking her exit was neither some new monster nor a stranger. It was Tom Lawson.

"Tom!" she shouted. "Get out of the way! Run!"

For a second, Tom's eyes flicked past her to take in whatever he saw through the far door to Alex's private office.

And then—without warning and without hesitation—he punched her right in the jaw.

He weighed nearly 200 pounds. Shelley was half that. Her eyes rolled up into their sockets and she was unconscious before she even started to fall.

17

Shelley came groggily to life, who knew how long later, to find she was propped up in a chair.

That wasn't so bad.

But she was also bound tightly in place by duct tape that was wrapped, with a thoroughness bordering on the obsessive, around her body and the chair.

That wasn't so good.

And her jaw hurt like a mofo, and another piece of tape was pulled tight across her mouth.

That was seriously fucked.

Worse, for one terrible timeless second, Shelley's body decided that it couldn't breathe through her nose and told her she was going to suffocate right there and then. Her eyes opened wide in growing panic and she began to struggle—uselessly—against her bonds. All she did was make the chair rattle on the floor.

"Be right with you," called Tom.

The tiny blessing in that was that hearing the bastard's voice distracted her enough to let breathing become again the autonomic response it needed to be and she realized that she wasn't going to die. At least not that second, and not from suffocation.

The chair to which he'd taped her was in the middle of the group study room. All the lights had been turned on in there, presumably by Tom. His voice, though, had come from Alex's private office.

Moontown

The chair wasn't facing the office and Shelley had to strain her eyes to the extreme corners of their sockets to try and look through the still open door.

Alex's corpse was still there. Just lying back limply in its chair where the only thing it was doing was, presumably, starting to go about the slow business of decomposition.

Tom was indeed in there with it. And he was being remarkably busy.

He was taking photographs of the dead doctor, and he was being very thorough about it—long shots, head shots, close-ups, profiles, all conceivable angles.

Shelley stared at him, almost as confused as she was horrified, watching as he dropped to one knee, canting his camera to take an arty low-angle shot of the dead body.

"Very nice…" Tom murmured, in what Shelley hoped was self-praise rather than encouragement to his model.

As if sensing her gaze, Tom looked at her across the distance between them. He raised his camera to her in a ridiculously normal gesture of explanation, as if he felt a gentlemanly need to apologize for keeping her waiting.

"Thought I'd catch a few shots of the good doctor while you were sleeping," he said.

Sleeping? Yeah, that was one way of putting it.

He straightened up and walked out of the office into the group study room and across to her. As he got nearer, he squinted to look at her face, his expression nothing but appraising and sympathetic.

"How's the jaw, by the way?" he said.

Right, like she could answer. She fixed her eyes on him and tried to keep anger out of the mix of emotions he might read there, thought it better to just let him see fear and confusion.

Wasn't difficult.

Tom moved to a position directly in front of her and stopped. He raised his camera.

"Smile," he said.

Flash! He took a picture of her.

Flash! Another.

Flash! And another.

Shelley felt her body jerk in shock with each successive flash as if they were almost painful. She steeled herself for another, but apparently three were enough.

"Okay," Tom said, "the pictures are done. Time for the next stage."

He put the camera away in one of the pockets of his jacket and reached into another for something else.

Shelley moaned behind her duct tape gag and felt her eyes growing wider. What was he reaching for? A knife? A gun? Something more unpleasantly inventive? She struggled again in the chair, just as uselessly as before.

But all he produced from the pocket was a small digital voice recorder. Pressing the record button, he leaned forward and yanked the tape from Shelley's mouth.

"Alright, then," he said, "tell me about the killings, Shelley. Tell me why you did it."

His voice was friendly. Hopeful, even. Nothing about it to suggest that he was kidding. For an incredulous moment or two, Shelley could only stare at him, her confusion deepening by the second.

"What?" she eventually managed.

Tom raised a hand. "Hold it a minute," he said. He clicked his little machine into playback mode and Shelley heard a tinny echo of her own voice and its disbelieving *what*.

Moontown

Tom pressed the record button again. "Okay," he said. "Levels are good. Go ahead."

"What the hell are you talking about?" she said, and her voice was neither angry nor defiant. She was asking an honest question. She really had no idea what he was talking about and she really wanted to know.

Tom gave her a tired look, the kind of look that a busy cop might give a dead-to-rights suspect who was insisting on wasting his time with a pretense of ignorance. "I think you know what I'm talking about, Shelley," he said. "I'm talking about a bunch of dead people. Anthony, Margaret, Doctor Drayton—sorry, *Alex*—and I'd like to know why you killed them."

As he threw out that list of the lost with a disgusting casualness that was almost sociopathic, everything else dropped away for Shelley except the one name on it that was new to her.

"Margaret?" she said, her voice sounding not disbelieving but simply small and reluctant, as if by not being heard it could somehow delay any confirming answer, make it not yet true.

"Oh, like you hadn't heard?" Tom said, with both a dismissal of what he plainly assumed to be her disingenuousness and a sneaking admiration for how convincingly she sold it. Then another thought seemed to occur to him. "My God," he said. "Are you actually *blanking* this stuff? Maybe you are! I hadn't even thought of that."

There was nothing in his voice to suggest he was kidding. Shelley stared at him in blank incredulity. The reality of her current situation came rushing back to her and any grief she would feel for Margaret was put on pragmatic hold. In its place came a furious anger that she could no longer contain despite the risk of expressing it to a man who was crazy enough to have knocked her out and tied her to a chair.

"I didn't kill *anybody*, you fucking psycho!" she yelled at him. "It's…oh my God…it's *you*! You killed them, didn't you?"

"Oh, that's good," Tom said, nodding with a slight smile. And again with the fucking *admiration* in his voice.

"*What's* good, asshole?" she said. Because she could try and guess what tone and attitude he wanted from her and try to give it to him in the hope that it might keep her safer longer. But the guy was, you know, fucking *nuts*, so who knew what would do what? Any little ersatz Stockholm Syndrome could kiss her white ass. *Deux fois.*

"Going straight to Plan B," he said, in answer to her question and clearly not phased at all by her aggression. "Finger another suspect. Classic. But it just isn't going to wash. Sorry. My times and movements have been rigorously accounted for. Rigorously. I was in a meeting when Anthony died, Margaret got creamed by a truck in front of half the damn city, and I was on the phone with my editor while you were doing Drayton."

"Your…*editor*?" she said. Well, he was just full of frickin' surprises, wasn't he?

"I'm an investigative journalist," he said—a little disappointed, like she should've figured that out by now. "I was working on an exposé about this whole bullshit confrontational-therapy thing and the late lamented Doc Drayton. *Much* bigger story now." He paused, gave her a faux apologetic look. "Oh, sorry about all that I'm-a-klepto crap, by the way," he said. "Cover story. You know, got me into the group."

She believed him immediately.

And equally as immediately felt much much worse.

She hadn't had time to process it all properly but she had, she now realized, been back-brain assuming for the last few minutes that this fucking lunatic had somehow been behind it all, even—in some absurd pre-rigged Rube Goldberg way—the insane stuff, the nightmare puppet show with Alex's corpse.

But if he was now telling her the truth, then who...what...

Her eyes flicked nervously around the room.

Tom seemed not to notice the change that had come over her. Why would he? He had no idea what she was thinking. Shit, *she* had no idea what she was thinking. She *wasn't* thinking yet. She was just feeling. And what she was feeling was very very afraid.

"So look," Tom said, blithely assuming that he was still in control of the situation. "*I* confessed. Your turn."

Shelley forced herself to speak as calmly as she possibly could, even tried for a small smile. "Untie me, Tom," she said. "Please."

"Oh, I don't think so," he said. "I may have got one lucky punch in, but Grandma Lawson taught me three things: Always eat your greens; wear a coat in winter; and don't fuck around with serial killers."

"I'm not a killer, Tom," she said, still doing her best to keep her voice quiet and reasonable and non threatening. "I swear it. And if you're not either, then we're both in danger. Real danger. Honestly. So, please—cut me loose and let's both get out of here."

Tom sighed. "This is going to make for very dull copy, Shelley," he said.

Shelley tried to fight down her rising panic. Fuck, she was going to have to engage with the dickhead, form a bond as fast as she could. She took a deep breath. "Who do you write for?" she said, in a voice she realized, with a tiny spasm of self-disgust, that she was borrowing from Verity Packwood, 12th grade Heather of her high school past. *Sure I'm a cheerleader*, the voice implied, *but nerds make me* so *hot*.

"PrettyStrangeDotCom," he said.

Shelley managed to hide the groan, but the Verity voice was out the window and taking its cocktease self back to 2002 and the first available quarterback. "A *website*?" she said.

"Hey," he said, stung. "The net is a perfectly valid forum for—"

"Don't get defensive, for Christ's sake!" she snapped, the urgency surfacing despite herself. "We don't have the time!"

"Then start talking."

"Look," she said, almost pleading now, "there's something going *on* here, something you don't understand. I don't understand it either, but—"

A sudden sound came from Alex's office.

Click-click-click. Like a cartoon crab clicking its claws.

"What was that?" Shelley said, and now the alarm in her voice was naked and fully exposed.

"What was what?" Tom said.

The sound had stopped. But there was no stopping the fear growing inside her. "There's a bigger story here," she said. "Much bigger. I'll help you break it. I promise. We can talk about it! Just get me out of here!" She rattled in the chair, struggling frustratedly inside her bonds.

Tom sighed again, the sigh of a man determined to stay patient in the face of stubborn hysteria but finding himself losing the struggle. "The sooner you talk," he said, "the sooner I'll—"

The lights in the group study room all went out.

Shelley gasped in the sudden darkness.

"What the fuck?" said Tom. And would have said more, but he was interrupted.

Echoing throughout the darkened room, seeming to have no specific point of origin but targeting on Tom with a subtle and dangerous delight, a male voice spoke.

"Tommy," it said. *"How I've missed you."*

Shelley couldn't tell where the voice was coming from—everywhere, nowhere—but she could see the devastating effect the mere sound of it had on Tom Lawson. He literally staggered in shock, the way someone would stagger when, having run wildly and windingly to evade a bully, a murderer, a monster, they turn the last corner of their escape route to find the bully / the murderer / the monster standing right there waiting for them.

"No!" he cried out, so instinctively and helplessly that Shelley wasn't even sure he knew he'd done it.

Her eyes were adjusting to the darkness—or perhaps it was just that the moonlight sneaking through the room's blinds was becoming stronger and brighter—and she could see Tom spinning around wildly, as if trying to locate the voice.

"Cut me loose!" she shouted at him.

"Shut up!" he shouted back. "Shut up!"

Shelley struggled more violently than ever against the binding tape, rattling her chair furiously.

"Cut me loose!" she yelled again. Louder. More desperately.

Tom just kept twisting around—until he stopped, jerking in fright and gasping at the sudden sight of a child in the darkness.

Shelley saw it too, and saw sooner than him that it was only a reflection in the room's wall-mirror. A reflection of a much younger Tom Lawson, a reflection of Tom Lawson as a child.

Shelley stopped breathing, felt herself go cold. It was just like what Anthony—and she—had seen in his fear-memory in the room at the rear of the abandoned garment factory. And, just like that earlier vision, this reflection was matching Tom's startled and frightened movements exactly.

"What's going on?" Tom said.

"It's your fear!" Shelley started to say. "Your mem—"

"What are you *doing*?!" he screamed. At *her*. And Shelley saw that he was suddenly staring at her in a mix of incredulous fear and furious anger. He rushed toward her. "What are you doing to me?!"

He grabbed her, far from gently, by the shoulders and Shelley braced herself for violence, but if it came she didn't feel it because instead, as soon as he made physical contact with her, she felt herself sliding instantly and helplessly into his recovering memory…

*

…and she was looking up from some low angle, like that of a child crouched on a floor, towards a towering vaulted ceiling.

Below the ceiling, filling as much of the stone wall spaces as possible, were an overwhelming number of massive icons and crucifixes.

In the distance, wooden spiral staircases led to overhanging choir galleries.

Moontown

Huge stained glass windows, at bizarrely canted angles, depicted the tortured martyrdom of misshapen Saints.

She had enough of her own consciousness left to wonder how real any of this nightmare mix of the Gothic and the Expressionist could ever have been. It was like High Mass was about to be celebrated on a redressed set from The Cabinet of Dr. Caligari.

She had no doubt that there'd been a church in Tom's youth.

She had no doubt that it hadn't looked like this.

She had no doubt that this was precisely how it had felt.

A figure in a full black robe was walking implacably toward her dreaming eyes. He might almost have been some nightmare version of a priest, except that she recognized him from Taylor's trading cards.

King Shadow halted, framed between two massive crucifixes of an ornate cruelty excessive even for medieval Catholicism, and looked down at her, him, them.

"One more game, Tommy," King Shadow said, and he raised his arms within his gown, which spread around him like the unfurling wings of a great black bird. "One more game."

The wooden heads of the crucified Christs turned to fix Shelley's dreaming eyes with their blank painted gaze. Fresh blood began to pour from their crowns of thorns. Their wooden mouths twitched into madman leers...

*

Tom staggered back from Shelley, breaking the memory-contact, and she watched in horrified pity as he shrank in on himself in the darkened group study room, his voice a childlike whimper.

"No," he was saying. "No, I don't want to. I don't want to...."

Shelley, still shaken by the violence and suddenness of the shared memory, needed to take a second or two to fight off the dizziness it had left in her but still managed to find her voice.

"Tom! It's not real!" she shouted at him. "Don't give in to it! It's not real!"

But it *was* real.

As Shelley watched, forced past disbelief to a simple numb horror, she saw that something terrible and inexplicable was happening to the darkness within the room.

Like an explosion seen in slo-mo and reverse, the darkness was beginning to *move*. To move inward, to coalesce into a central core. And however impossible it may have been, Shelley felt, sensed, *knew* that the darkness was moving not by accident but by intent.

The shadows deepened around Tom, gathering eagerly about him like a thickening and sentient black fog until he was lost to sight inside what appeared to be an almost solid box of darkness.

Lost to sight. But not to sound.

Terrible noises came from deep inside the impenetrable walls of the pulsing core of shadow in front of Shelley: a symphonic cacophony of whipping, tearing, and rending sounds, accompanied by agonized human screams and an utterly inhuman and hideously triumphant laughter.

Shelley, distraught and terrified, rocked violently in her chair, screaming at the darkness. "Stop it! Stop it! Let him go!"

Despite her pleas, the nightmare noises continued, increasing in volume and severity until, having built to a crescendo of torment, they suddenly cut off completely, leaving only a ringing echo in the room.

Moontown

Shelley froze in place, staring in appalled horror at the solid core of blackness. As the terminal echo finally dissipated, there was a beat or two of silence and then the sound of something wet and limp dropping heavily to the floor.

Shelley's voice was tiny and frightened. "Tom?" she said, without hope or expectation, feeling the pointlessness of saying it but having to say it anyway.

As if in response, the dense gathering of gelid shadow began to melt away back into loose and swirling clouds of a still-heavy pitch-black fog and, dimly visible through the rolling black mists, two figures were slowly revealed to Shelley's eyes.

One—the one that was curled in a loose-limbed mass on the floor—was Tom. Or what used to be Tom. There could be little doubt that all life had left that twisted and tortured body. Shelley said nothing, practically *felt* nothing, was past any response other than an almost unconscious sobbing.

The other figure—standing amid the rolling darkness almost as if part of it—looked like a powerfully built man, looked human.

But Shelley knew better.

At first, it was in the shape that had come out of his lost memory for Tom Lawson, its King Shadow incarnation, swathed in its black and winglike robes. But as Shelley watched—beyond words, beyond thought, beyond feeling—it took on its other personae sequentially, as if in some kind of darkly celebratory display.

As the black mists played over it, alternately hiding and revealing it, the thing that had stepped into the world shifted its appearance gleefully like some quick-change clown in Hell's vaudeville. Shelley saw those creatures she had seen as painted cards in her earlier dream journey flick before her undreaming eyes one after another in rapid and awful succession until finally, as the black clouds at last dissipated into nothingness, the figure took on the shape and appearance of the first of its selves that Shelley had seen as an adult.

The Ragman stood before her, his dark eyes glinting in unholy pleasure as he watched her cringe at the sight of him, her eyes widening in awestruck terror.

Shelley felt her lips move, heard herself mumbling, had no idea what she was saying or trying to say, knew only that it was a babbling litany of meaningless denial and pointless disbelief.

For a moment, the monster just stood there, looking down at her, bound and helpless.

And then he moved.

Shelley gasped.

But all he did was to spread his arms and to take an elaborate and theatrical bow, slow, sure, and graceful.

As he straightened up elegantly from the bow, Shelley stared at him, confusion now added to the cocktail of terror and wonder that was racing through her blood. She tried to say something, tried to find words, tried to pretend that conversation was possible with something so overwhelmingly *other*.

The Ragman raised a finger to his lips.

"Shhh," he said softly.

He closed the distance between them with the terrifying speed she remembered from Anthony's memory. She flinched but, again, was surprised by what the creature did. He stopped short of her chair, and then crouched in front of her.

"Shelley," he said, in a tone of what would almost be called affection were such a dreadful voice capable of it. "You were always my favorite."

He drew something from within the multicolored motley he wore and then looked into her eyes.

"I couldn't have done it without you," he said, and Shelley looked down, horrified in a completely new way, as he slipped the ring onto her helpless finger.

Set within a simple silver band, the jewel was a richly hued moonstone. It held Shelley's uncomprehending gaze for a moment or two, seeming to completely fill her field of vision...

And suddenly the lights were all back on in the group study room and the monster was nowhere to be seen.

Shelley was completely alone.

Apart from the corpses of Alex and Tom, of course.

And the ring on her finger.

She dropped her head for a moment in a mix of relief, confusion, and utter exhaustion—until the startling sound of an electronic crackle made her jerk it up again, with a gasp of renewed fear.

But it was okay. Well, you know, as okay as it could be under the circumstances.

The crackle was just the static burst of the walkie-talkie in the hand of a security guard who was standing in the main doorway of the room, staring in disbelief at what he saw in there and in the office beyond; the dead bodies of the men and the bound and helpless Shelley.

He lifted the walkie to his face and spoke into it. "We're gonna need a couple black-and-whites out here," he said.

For one ridiculous second, Shelley thought he was ordering malts for them both until she realized he meant police cars. She thought maybe she'd laugh but instead, as the guard started walking into the room towards her, her body finally allowed her to faint.

18

The room was small and square and featureless and, though its walls weren't actually padded, their antiseptic whiteness, along with the room's relative absence of furnishings, would certainly suggest to anyone who saw it that Shelley had been brought to a place reserved for the mentally suspect.

She looked across the small white table to the white-coated man who sat opposite her. He'd been talking for quite a while now and, despite Shelley's monosyllabic and guarded replies, seemed happy to keep talking.

"Let's be clear," he said now. "You're hardly a suspect in all this—it's obvious that you couldn't have bound yourself to that chair in that particular manner—so tell me again what's wrong with the scenario that this Tom Lawson fellow murdered everyone and then died of a heart attack?"

"Because it isn't true," Shelley said, and made no attempt to hide the aggressive contempt in her voice.

The man in the white coat smiled. "But I can take it, can I, that you nevertheless see that *your* reading of the situation poses a certain question of... credibility?"

"Yes."

"May I summarize your interpretation?"

"Knock yourself out."

"You believe that your empathetic abilities, fed and reinforced by the buried fears of your clients, have somehow channeled into corporeal existence a... what?... a supernatural being?"

Moontown

"Yes."

"A supernatural being who haunts—has *always* haunted—the collective unconscious of children, but who has now, with your unwitting and unwilling help, stepped—somewhat gleefully in your view—into the real world."

"Yes."

"Hmm," he said, and looked at her appraisingly.

19

Out the window from which Taylor used to like to stare at the world and its mysteries, Molly Edwards could see the two parked police cars—parked illegally as it happened, but who were you going to call?—on the far side of the campus quad.

In the middle of the quad itself, she saw one of the uniformed cops talking with one of the detectives, the latter making notes, the uniform pointing to the road beyond.

It was a lovely day, Molly noted, a glorious combination of the sunlight that Angelenos could take for granted most days of the year and that special crisp clarity that came much less often but made October in southern California so spectacular when it did. Molly wished that the day had been cold and gray and miserable. The beauty of the fall weather just seemed pointlessly cruel to her. It made what had happened—what was still happening—seem even more unlikely and unpleasant.

Inside the group study room, a couple of post-grad TAs had been roped in to help another of the uniformed cops escort all the kids out of the building to wherever the various vehicles were waiting to take them home.

The kids were streaming past Molly as she stood near her desk with the two other detectives. As if reading her mood, hardly any of the kids were looking at her, let alone saying good-bye.

Molly looked away from the window and back to the detectives. "And his parents didn't see anything?" she said.

Moontown

The first detective, the one that looked a bit like that guy that used to be on *The Dick Van Dyke Show*—not Morey Amsterdam, the bald one—shook his head. "Just an empty bed," he said.

"This is awful," Molly said. Like it needed saying. "And you really think somebody took him?"

The other detective, the younger slicker one, the one that you could kind of tell was, like, *into* being a detective, said "We're still gathering information, Ma'am."

Molly nodded, though she really had no idea what her nod meant. "Taylor's been … upset … lately," she said. "But I—"

At the sound of Taylor's name, Audrey—who was the last of the kids to be herded out past them—looked up at Molly and interrupted her.

"Taylor went away," she said.

Molly and the detectives all looked down at her. The bald detective gave a quick hand signal to the uniform in charge of the kids' exodus to tell him to hold up for a minute.

Molly crouched down to be at eye-level with Audrey. "Audrey?" she said. "Do you know where Taylor went?"

Audrey nodded but looked up guardedly at the two strangers who were standing with Ms. Edwards as if nervous or unwilling to speak in their presence.

"It's alright, Audrey," Molly said, stroking gently at the girl's arm to reassure her that everything was okay, that they were just having a conversation. "Could you tell me where he went, sweetie?"

"He got in the car," said Audrey.

From the edge of her vision, Molly saw the quick this-isn't-good look that passed between the two detectives but she tried not to let it distract her.

"The car?" she said to Audrey.

Audrey nodded.

"And the car took Taylor away?"

Audrey nodded.

"Did you see who was driving the car, sweetheart?"

Audrey nodded.

"Had you ever seen the person who was driving before?"

Audrey gave Molly a look, an oddly grownup kind of look, a look that, had Audrey not been seven years old and sweet as they come, could only have been translated as *are you shittin' me?*

"Of course," she said.

Molly looked at her, which seemed to be prompt enough for Audrey to clarify. "It was Ms. Campbell," she said.

Molly didn't ask Audrey if she was sure. She could tell that she was sure. She could tell that Audrey had no doubt in her mind that she had seen Shelley Campbell put Taylor in her car and drive him away somewhere.

"You know that person, ma'am?" said the second detective.

Molly nodded, standing up. "Let's let Audrey get home, shall we?" she said, looking at the older of the detectives. He nodded, and waved a go-ahead to the uniform.

Audrey went with the cop without a complaint. "Bye, Ms. Edwards," she said brightly over her shoulder and then, almost as an afterthought and again with a curious maturity seemingly beyond her years, "I'm sure everything's going to be fine."

Molly looked back at the little girl as she said it and saw that Audrey was looking not at her but instead directly across the room at the plastic playhouse.

As the door closed behind Audrey and the uniformed cop,

Molly too stared over at the playhouse, at its wide open door and its empty interior.

*

Taylor Smith wasn't very happy about being back inside the playhouse.

Even though Ms. Campbell was in there with him, hunkered down in a tight cramped fit on account of her being a grownup and all, he didn't feel very safe.

"It's okay, Taylor," Ms. Campbell said, as if she could tell how he was feeling. "I'm here with you."

Taylor nodded in what he hoped was a brave way, but he figured the look in his eyes was probably still letting her know that he was very unsure about this.

He took a look past the playhouse's closed plastic door and out its circular window and was reassured a little to find that all he could see through it was their classroom. He kind of wished other people had been in the classroom—so that other people would know where he and Ms. Campbell were, just in case—but, even though the classroom was completely empty, it was at least the classroom and not that other place of shadowed hills and roads down which the bad thing came.

*

The Freeway Motel—and was ever a just-off-the-interstate fleabag motel named so honestly and unpretentiously?—had only twenty-four rooms to offer travelers, twelve upstairs twelve downstairs, and nothing in the way of other facilities unless you counted the parking lot as an extra.

Inside room seven the thin curtains, drawn over the single large plate-glass window, were doing a spectacularly bad job of keeping out the day's sunlight.

The room itself was as anonymous and cookie-cutter a cheap motel room as anyone could ask for: a simple rectangular box design, the rear quarter of its inelegant space given over to a tiny en suite bathroom, with nothing in the way of amenities in the room proper other than a single table and chair, a television set that was literally bolted to the wall to discourage theft—because, who knows, there might one day be a hot collector's market for seventeen-inch nonflat-screen tube-driven dinosaurs—and a single, albeit king-size, bed.

On the bed, fully dressed and on top of the covers, Shelley Campbell and Taylor Smith were lying beside each other asleep.

Shelley's left hand was wrapped protectively around the little boy's right, and their eyes, twitching in REM rapidity beneath their closed lids, moved in a curious synchronicity, each pair matching every slide and shiver of the other.

*

Inside the playhouse, inside Taylor's memory, Shelley—along for the ride just as she had been with Anthony and Margaret and, briefly and unwillingly, Tom Lawson—looked past Taylor's nervous face to the rear wall of the cramped plastic space.

Just as he'd told her there would be, there was another door in the rear wall, a door that Shelley knew perfectly well didn't exist in the real world's version of the playhouse.

"Through here?" she asked him, gesturing at the door.

Moontown

Taylor nodded, a little reluctantly, and Shelley gave him a smile that was as encouraging and confident as she could make it before pushing the door open and squeezing through.

Followed by the boy, Shelley made her way down the bizarre red plastic stairs—sturdy enough, surprisingly, given their building materials and their, you know, non-fucking-existence—and then walked briskly along the equally odd and unsettling yellow plastic corridor until she reached the door at the end of the corridor.

Giving Taylor another reassuring smile—*fake it till you make it*, she thought, remembering an acting class mantra that some friend minoring in Theater Arts had passed on to her—she took hold of his hand again and opened the door.

They emerged into the nightscape of the children's playground, with its moonlit-bathed swings and sandboxes and the welcoming-but-not-really *Jimmy Midnight's Garden of Delights* sign.

She felt Taylor clinging to her hand particularly tightly as his nervous eyes swept the sandboxes for any occupants of the sad and pale persuasion. He'd told her about the little dead children with the long nails on their clandestine drive to the Freeway Motel, and she had no desire for him to have to see them again. That's why she wanted to move as fast as they could, before this place and its master, rather than she, could begin setting the agenda.

"Be brave, Taylor," she said. Yeah. Big talk, Shell. "I just need to know where we are...."

As she spoke, she was walking them both to the top of one of the playground's small grassy rises. From there, she could look down at the surrounding landscape.

She'd expected to see it, but there was nevertheless a stiletto-precise stab of fear in her heart as she saw, in the midnight distance beyond the shadowed hills, a long narrow two-lane blacktop cutting through the flatlands to disappear into the horizon.

She almost wouldn't have been surprised to see her old car speeding along it. It was the road from the nightmare version of her car crash, the road where black-clad, shadow-featured hitchers would not be denied their ride.

20

In the white room, across the table from Shelley, the man in the white coat had some more questions.

"So your belief, correct me if I'm wrong, is that everybody's fear is essentially the *same* fear?"

"No," said Shelley.

"Little help here?"

Shelley had no desire at all to help him. But she did want to help herself, help herself to understand at least, and it wasn't like she'd yet really had time to articulate, or even to formulate in her mind, what it was precisely that she *was* thinking.

"Our memories," she said, "our *dreams* of our memories, it's like they're all...connected."

She paused, like she knew that wasn't quite right. The man in the white coat looked at her, and she thought she saw the tiniest suggestion in his eyes that he too knew that wasn't exactly it but that he was more than prepared to be patient with her.

"No," she said, trying again. "Not connected. Or not *just* connected. It's more like that they—I mean, however individuated—that they all take place in...another country. That, together, they *form* another country...a dream country...I—"

"Ah," the man in the white coat said, as if he couldn't resist interrupting her any longer. He nodded too, like he approved of where this was going. "A dream country.

Very good. Many aboriginal cultures believe that, whatever anyone dreams, everyone dreams in the same *place*. Believe further that that place is perfectly *real*, it's just... somewhere else."

Shelley nodded. "That sounds right. But I'm talking about something specific. I'm saying that in that dream country there's a special territory. An awful one. A place of endless night, ruled by the moon. A place where all fears live."

"Interesting," he said. "Very interesting." And he sat back to look at her. As if she wasn't crazy at all, as if he were pleased with her progress.

21

In the moonlit playground, atop the incongruously gentle rise of the landscaped hillock, Shelley pulled her eyes away from the long narrow blacktop in the distant flatlands and turned to look back down the hill.

At the bottom of the rise, just outside the white perimeter fence that sectioned off the playground, there was a wooden directional sign-post, one of the old-fashioned types, complete with a carved pointing finger.

It read *Moontown*, and Shelley was pretty damn sure that it hadn't been there earlier. It wasn't as if that sort of thing—*now you don't see it, now you do*—wasn't to be expected to happen in a place such as this, but the fact that something *had* happened meant that their presence here was now known. Something had opened an eye and seen them, taken a breath and smelled them, cocked an ear and—fuck it, pick whatever frickin' metaphor you want, Moontown and its master were now aware that they had come and were preparing, perhaps leisurely, perhaps not, to begin a response.

Shelley risked one more moment to look across and down in the direction the sign pointed, and saw that below and beyond the playground was a much bigger place. It too, like the signpost, might only just have manifested itself but Shelley actually felt that it had been there all along, that it was the permanent heart of this territory and that if it had seemed invisible earlier it was more a question of the sentient selectivity of the overhead moon as to where it shone its cold blue light, which had now spread, in perverse generosity, from the playground alone to the surrounding neighborhood.

It was like a movie-set version of a classic American small town. Not even that, really, more just a small town's Main Street. There were no lights in its buildings and it appeared to be deserted.

But Shelley didn't need, or couldn't afford, to take in more than this first glance right now. Not while the boy was still here.

She turned back to Taylor, knelt in front of him, and spoke to him in a clear and firm voice.

"Taylor," she said, "you're such a brave boy, and I thank you very much for getting me here. Now—remember when we talked before we went to sleep?"

Taylor nodded, his eyes fixed on Shelley's. Behind the fear, there was a glint of trust that melted her heart.

"Remember that I told you that there was a special word? A safe word?"

Again, a nod.

"Yellow," said Shelley, her voice clear, confident, and distinct.

And Taylor vanished.

*

In room seven of the Freeway Motel, Taylor Smith jerked upright on the king-size bed, his eyes wide open.

He looked down at Ms. Campbell, who was still asleep just like she'd told him she would be, and then he got off the bed and crossed the room to the table and chair, where a juice drink, a bag of chips, and the TV remote were waiting for him.

Moontown

He looked back at Ms. Campbell before he sat down, just to check, but she'd said it might be a while before she woke up too, so he opened the bag of chips, turned on the TV, and settled in to wait.

*

The moment Taylor disappeared, Shelley felt her mind assaulted as if in some kind of revenge attack, as if the power that held dominion here was lashing out angrily in response to an action of which it did not approve.

It lasted only a few seconds, but was more than a little disconcerting because, even though Shelley was already within a dreamscape, it was as if she was suddenly and involuntarily forced into another dream, or a dream within a dream. At first she could see nothing at all, like a dream of being blind. More than blind: trapped in a lightless void with no sense of her own body at all. The only sensory impression, in fact, was sound. There was music playing. Unpleasant music.

Lilting but dissonant, the disturbed melody sounded almost familiar to her—as if a well-known carnival tune had been transposed to a minor key, perhaps, or as if some wiseass had taken a half-remembered nursery rhyme and remixed it for a block party in Dante's ninth circle.

Shelley might have tried to identify it but an image claimed her attention, single and distinct, swelling up from the all-encompassing darkness like flotsam from an otherwise invisible sea of dreams. It was a child's crayon drawing, colorful and frantic, its awkward and anguished lines portraying a hulking figure emerging gleefully from confinement like a madman stepping out of a midnight closet.

Almost as soon as it appeared, the image sank back into the lightless deep and the music drowned with it, the final disappearing notes sounding almost like words, as if a calliope larynx, distant and echoed, was trying to say *remember me*.

And then the moment was over and the world came back —well, *this* world at least—and Shelley was again standing on the crest of the playground's hill beneath the huge and heavy full moon.

The moon's blue and silver face, she noticed for the first time, not only dominated the night sky but was literally the only thing in it. The sky was both cloudless and starless, a combination of absences that was much odder and more unsettling than she would have thought it would be had somebody merely described it to her.

She had another thought too, a better one.

What had just happened to her—the dream within the dream or whatever—might not in fact have been an attack at all, or at least not a conscious one. In retrospect, it felt more like it had been an unthinking animal response, like the automatic twitch of a nerve.

In other words, this place hadn't done it to *her* so much as she had forced that response out of *it*. As if her getting Taylor out of there had been so much something it hadn't expected—or, even better, hadn't understood—that it had…what?…had actually *blinked*? Or even, please God, flinched.

Perhaps she'd frightened it, Shelley thought, and allowed herself a brief moment of pleasure at that possibility of the biter bit. She wasn't going to count *those* chickens yet, but there was something else: if it *had* been a blink, if that brief disappearance of all this...fucking *landscaping*...was something that had happened to it, not to her, then that at least suggested a vulnerability to its hold on its own territories that she hadn't before dared to presume, suggested that perhaps its pretty and baroque constructs were as fragile in their own way as the gossamer inventions of any human dream.

Boy, that felt great for a minute.

And the thought of quitting while she was ahead was dangerously tempting.

But she knew she wasn't going to do that, and she also knew that, while she was here, basking in microscopic victories for more than a second or two was tantamount to letting her guard down, and that was something she couldn't risk doing. Because she *was* still here. In its territory, not hers. And nothing was blinking now.

Below her, below the playground's hills, the dream town's dusty thoroughfare was waiting for her. It was lined on either side by the unlit buildings, which she'd noticed before, and their garishly painted wooden hoardings, which she hadn't. Each of the hoardings was unreadable in the moonlight, at least from this distance. Something looked wrong about the place—*well, thank you and* duh, *Little Miss State the Fucking Obvious*—like it was an uneasy conflation of two carelessly remembered realities; half-small town Main Street, half-carnival Midway. Yeah, like it cared if its design wasn't seamless. All the better to eat you with, my dear.

Well, standing here wasn't going to get the crops watered or the critters fed, so Shelley started down the hill. Like she'd traded in her sanity for a pair of big brass balls.

As she got closer to the main drag, she saw that the buildings looked not only unlit but long abandoned. There was what might have been a church, its tall stained-glass windows unilluminated now, and, a little further along, something that could once have been an Old West saloon, to judge by its creakily swinging wooden doors.

At the far end of the strip, squaring it off—you know, where the town hall would be if you were in Mayberry—was a hulking building that reminded Shelley of a derelict movie theater. Over its big double doors, where the marquee might once have been, was another of the large wooden hoardings. This one she could read, now that she was at the bottom of the hill and starting along the street itself.

The Funhouse, it said. Huh. Shelley had her doubts. Gazing at it made her feel uncomfortable—well, you know, *more* uncomfortable—as if it was stabbing at a memory of something unpleasant that had once happened to her there, even though she knew she had never seen it before.

The moon, which seemed to have a fine line in focal specificity, was now bathing the Funhouse in most of its light. Like a spotlight letting her know that this was where the action was. Like it was beckoning her.

She'd certainly felt better about come-ons but, in a weird way, she was almost grateful for this apparent declaration of venue because it allowed her to feel a little less like something might happen before she got there, allowed her to feel safer —marginally safer—as she made her way towards it down the rest of Main Street, as she passed each of the other empty and abandoned buildings.

There was a gap between two of the structures. Not a side street, not really, more like the mouth of an alley. Shelley had no desire to do any extra exploring, but she did risk a glance down the alley. In the far distance, on what would have been the outskirts of town had the town actually been a town, there was a single large building. Shelley'd never seen it from the outside before, but she knew immediately what it was. It was the abandoned garment factory where Anthony had run from the darkness and the monster within it.

After the alley came the abandoned church and, as Shelley moved past it, light bloomed inside as if a thousand candles had been lit at once, illuminating the stained-glass windows. She recognized their surreal design from Tom's nightmare memory and tried not to look too closely as the distorted shadow of a dark robed figure was thrown by the candles onto one of the windows.

She still felt that paradoxical sense of poisoned safety, felt that anything she was shown here was just... *teasing*, was intended just to soften her up, to get her ready for her hot date in the Funhouse and that nothing was actually going to happen to her until she reached it. It wasn't just the moon's spotlighting of the building, of course. It was the fact that she was wearing the moonstone ring that the monster had slid onto her finger, marking her as his possession in some vile echo of a medieval warlord branding his bartered bride.

On the other side of the street, one of the saloon's wooden doors creaked, swinging in a sudden night wind. There was another sound too, an urgent clawlike skittering like that of a long-nailed animal moving fast to avoid being seen. Shelley looked down to the gutter that ran along the edge of the clapboard sidewalk on that side of the street just in time to see an oversized rat disappearing down a storm drain in front of the saloon. The rat's tail was long, absurdly and hideously long, more than twice its body length, and pink, segmented, and hairless.

As she looked back up from the gutter, she saw that the dead brother and sister that Taylor had told her about were standing in the saloon's doorway, their long black hair rippling around their faces as if something unseen was running its invisible fingers possessively through it. Shelley met their dark eyes for a second and then looked away, troubled not by the coldness of their gaze but by the fear that seemed to dance behind it.

Looking ahead, Shelley continued toward the Funhouse, feeling the children's lost eyes shift in their pale little faces to watch her go.

22

"This shared dreamscape," the man in the white coat said, as if he wanted to be fair, as if he wanted to get all the details right, "this place where all fears live..."

"Moontown," Shelley said, interrupting him.

"Oh," he said. "Catchy."

He allowed a nod of approval to slip through his professional mask before continuing.

"This *Moontown*," he said, "is the habitat, the natural environment, of the demon that you believe you've helped to unleash?"

"Yes."

"And who do you think *he* is?"

Shelley stared at him. There was a jaunty eagerness to that last question that she found particularly offensive. But she was ready to answer him.

"The monster under the bed," she said. "The boogeyman in the closet. The man—the *thing*—that our parents say isn't there in the dark."

"And does he have a *name*?"

"Many names," she said, "and the children know all of them."

"But the adults don't?"

"We grow up. We forget."

"And what? Just discard him?"

Shelley sneered across the table. "Dismiss him like a broken toy," she said.

23

The big double doors of the Funhouse, like those of many a derelict theater, had had their glass plates replaced by cheap plywood panels which were covered by fly-posted handbills and posters, yellowing with age. One in particular caught Shelley's eye:

DO THE DEAD SPEAK?

THE MOONGLOW SUPPER ROOM
IS PROUD TO PRESENT

*That celebrated exponent of the Ventriloquial arts
and explorer of the regions of the damned*

PROFESSOR ECHO

*Recently returned from his latest expedition to the Plutonian
depths and accompanied, for this engagement only, by the
comic stylings of those much-loved masters of mirth and mayhem*

MISTER SPONGE AND MISTER SCROTUM
TWO WHO SHOULD NEVER BE STRANGERS

Thrice nightly. When you least expect it.

There was graffiti too, some carved into the wood, some scribbled over the posters and announcements. Most were, as in the real world, simple puerile obscenities making sexual promises on which their authors would unlikely be able to deliver, but there were one or two that Shelley assumed, like the handbill from the Moonglow Supper Room, were there especially for her benefit. Just to, you know, make her feel at home. Such as the redolent phrase—scored deeply into the plywood in serrated scratchy letters as if written by talons—*gonna have some fun tonight*.

Yeah, well, enough with the coming attractions. Shelley was here for the feature presentation. She pushed the double-doors open and walked inside.

If the Funhouse had ever been a theater it had long been stripped of seats, screen, and lobby. Instead it was, as she might have guessed, a kind of indoor carnival, as if someone had taken a small amusement park or county fair and jammed it within the plain wooden walls of an amphitheater-like space, a space that was undeniably big but not so big that the various entertainments shoehorned in there didn't give an uncomfortable sense of jostling for position as if they were crammed together a little too close for comfort.

There were no windows in there, and the entire place was lit only by the scores of decorative but dusty string-lights that festooned almost everything. Some of the lights worked, many were out, and several flickered arrhythmically as if perfectly willing to die but in no hurry about it. It was like a sudden evacuation had been called at a carnival once upon a long ago midnight, and the last man out had forgotten to turn off the lights.

Rides, games, and machines were everywhere, all of them recognizable from their real-world analogues, but all of them subtly and unpleasantly different. The carousel horses, for example, were oversized and disproportioned and their painted expressions were cruel and fierce enough that Shelley didn't like to look at them.

Shelley weaved her way through a cramped aisle trying not to be distracted by the old-school popcorn machine, the glass-encased upper canopy of which was filled to overflowing with a huge pile of rotting kernels. The pile was pulsing and rippling, not from decay alone but also from the thousand cockroaches that swarmed within it.

Cheap shot, Shelley thought, but nevertheless felt an annoyingly overwhelming need to scratch wildly at her clothing and her hair and to move on more rapidly than before.

A skeletally framed Ghost Train car suddenly sputtered into life on its single-rail track and bashed open the doors to its ride, disappearing within. Before the doors closed behind the car, Shelley was fairly sure she caught a glimpse of a familiar black-coated figure standing some distance down the track in the darkness and waiting for his ride.

Massive ceiling-to-floor velvet curtains, their Victorian splendor surrendering to the damp-stained rot of mildew and mold, hung across the entire width of the Funhouse's back wall. Shelley made her way purposefully toward them.

Their draped heaviness parted easily in her hands, admitting her to a dark and narrow and unnaturally long corridor down both sides of which an apparently infinite series of doors ran before disappearing into the darkness.

Shelley made her way past several of the doors before deciding to stop. Fuck this pick-a-card, hide-and-seek shit. She called out into the darkness, fully confident that she would be heard.

Moontown

"What?" she said. "You expect me to toss a coin?"

One of the doors beside her cracked open, emitting a narrow band of bright white light.

Shelley took a moment, took a breath, opened the door wider and walked through it.

The room was small and square and featureless and, though its walls weren't actually padded, their antiseptic whiteness, along with the room's relative absence of furnishings, put Shelley in mind of a cell in a mental ward.

A figure in a white coat sat at the room's single table, his familiar deeply shadowed features smiling in welcome. Shelley crossed the room and sat down opposite the monster.

24

"And what? Just discard him?"

Shelley sneered across the table at him. "Dismiss him like a broken toy," she said. "Poor monster. Poor pathetic monster."

"Pathetic?" said the figure in the white coat, losing his smile. "Tell that to your dead friends."

He let that sink in a moment and then twisted the knife. "Or are you reluctant to raise the issue with them, given your assistance in their various leavings of the world?"

Shelley wanted to spit in his face. She was utterly astonished at how unafraid she felt. "All I did was to help people remember," she said. "And it wasn't the remembering that killed them. The remembering would have *freed* them. Freed them from the damage you'd done long before. No, it was you that killed them. What *I* did was let you thumb a fucking ride while I wasn't looking. But I'm looking now, looking right at you, and telling you that that won't be happening any more."

She pulled the moonstone ring from her finger and laid it on the table. "I'm returning your ring," she said. "This relationship isn't working."

Anger clouded the monster's face. The white light of the room suddenly dimmed and darkened, mutating into a bilious yellow like that of a dying gaslamp struggling through a globe smeared with the accrued grime of centuries. As when he had taken Tom Lawson, shadowed blackness began to swirl in mists around him and, within the dark fogs, his face seemed to slip and shift.

"I'll see your ring," he said, passing his hand over the table like a stage magician and from nowhere fanning out a face-down hand of cards, just like Taylor and Jen had shown her in the car, "and raise you five princes of darkness."

The dark mists deepened around him and, obscured within them, his body seemed just as mutable and as fluid as they, sliding into and out of each of its personae in turn.

Shelley chose not to be impressed. "Smoke and mirrors," she said. "You're a sideshow trick, a carnival freak. Well, it's time for the circus to pull out of town."

Inside the black mists, the creature shook its head. "I don't think so," it said. "Fear is a year-round attraction."

"I'm looking fear in the face and telling it it's full of shit," Shelley said. "You can stay here in your sad little chamber of horrors, but you're not using me to get to the real world anymore. I *forget* you. You hear me? I choose to forget you."

A mocking imitation of alarm came into the creature's voice. "I'm melting! I'm melting!" it said.

"That's about right," Shelley said, unfazed by his pretty good Margaret Hamilton imitation. "But I'm not Dorothy. I'm Alice. And you're nothing but a pack of cards."

There was no doubt in her voice nor, as she stared across the table at him, a trace of fear in her eyes.

The black mists began to dissipate. The yellow light gave way to white, which grew stronger and brighter with every passing moment.

Shelley, keeping her eyes fixed unwaveringly on his, reached her hand out across the table. "Game over," she said, and swept the cards from the table to the floor.

The figure on the other side of the table—smaller, slighter, less substantial by the second—had nothing further to say.

And then there was no table, no chair, nobody in the room but her. It wasn't even a room, just a limitless place of bright white light.

Shelley closed her eyes...

25

...and opened them again.

She sat up on the bed in room seven of the Freeway Motel.

Across the room, Taylor was watching the TV. He turned his head to look at her.

"Hi," he said casually and then glanced a little guiltily at the empty pack of chips on the table as if wondering too late if he was perhaps meant to have saved some for her.

"Hi," said Shelley. "What're you watching?"

"Cartoons," he said.

"Funny?"

Taylor shrugged. "Kinda."

"Taylor?" Shelley said, and her voice now was careful and searching. "It's over, sweetheart. The bad man's gone."

"'Kay," said Taylor. Like, you know, no biggie.

Shelley smiled. "Ready to go?"

"Sure."

*

She didn't let go of his hand until there was only one street left for him to cross.

Only when there was no traffic at all did she send him on his way and, from a vantage point on the opposite corner, watch as he walked up the stone steps to the front door of the police precinct.

And only when the door had closed safely behind him, did Shelley turn away and lose herself in the pedestrian traffic.

*

The counterman made his way down his side of the counter in the coffee shop, bearing the large Black and White Malt.

Shelley watched him come, relishing the moment.

"Enjoy," he said, setting the shake down in front of her and giving the space around it a half-hearted wipe with his towel.

"I better," said Shelley. "Could be my last for a while."

"Yeah?"

"I'll be going to prison."

The counterman looked at her quizzically.

Shelley nodded. "Kidnapping," she said. "Child endangerment." She paused, thought about it. "You better bring me a side of fries."

The counterman nodded—a little guardedly, a little confused, but an order was an order—and moved back down his side of the counter to the kitchen's serving hatch.

Shelley took a look out the coffee shop's big plate-glass window and watched the undergrads crisscrossing outside it for a moment before turning back to the counter, leaning in to her shake, and taking a long sweet mouthful from it. Do you *drink* something as satisfyingly thick as this, she thought idly, or do you *eat* it?

Whatever the answer, she was still savoring that first fabulous hit when a small noise—somewhere between a bark and a yelp—drew her eyes across the coffee shop floor to one of the booths.

Moontown

A woman—too old to be a student, too suburban-widow to be faculty—was surreptitiously feeding tiny pieces of her burger to her small lapdog, whose little fluffy white head was protruding from the woman's bag, which sat beside her plate on the Formica table top.

Shelley smiled at the sight and then turned back to the business of thoroughly enjoying her last shake. She'd meant what she'd said to the counterman. She knew she'd be doing time before very long. In fact, she had every intention of turning herself in once she was done here, because she was pretty sure that waiting for some APB responder to find her instead wouldn't help her case any. She noticed that a guy three stools down from her at the counter had been watching her watch the woman and her dog. He was holding a newspaper, which was folded back on itself so that it was open to the sports scores and which he'd presumably been reading when he was minding his own business.

"Cute, huh?" he said to her, nodding his head in the direction of the bagged dog.

Shelley nodded, hoping for no further conversation, and was relieved to see that the counterman was already heading back her way with her order of fries. He put the plate down beside her shake and pulled a ketchup container out from its chrome holder for her.

"Thanks," she said, and leaned in to her plate, trusting that the guy with the paper would leave her alone to eat. She'd downed a fry or three—not bad, but it wasn't like the Black and Whites were going to lose their status as the big draw here—before she became aware that the counterman hadn't left. He was still standing on his side of the counter directly in front of her.

Regretting her previous openness with him about her likely future situation—blame the adrenaline rush of, you know, vanquishing a demonic entity and all—and wondering if she could deflect his curiosity by pretending she'd just been kidding, she looked up at him and was surprised to see that it wasn't her he was interested in at all.

He was instead staring across the dining room in the direction of the booth where Shelley had seen the woman feeding her dog. And from the look on his face Shelley doubted that it was any issue of hygiene or health regulation that was bothering the counterman. His expression was one of utter terror.

"What's the matter?" Shelley said, already spinning around on her stool to see for herself.

The dog had crawled out of his owner's bag and was taking a little turn around the table. For such a small dog, he had a surprisingly long tail. It was pink, segmented, and hairless. The tail of an oversized rat.

"Haven't seen one like that since the funeral," said the guy three stools down.

Shelley turned to look down the counter at him. He was standing as if ready to leave and was folding his newspaper back out the right way so that the front page was visible.

"Whose funeral?" said Shelley.

"Mine," he said, real casual, and headed for the exit door.

He had tucked his folded newspaper under his arm—but not before Shelley had had an opportunity to read the front page banner headline.

In huge type—type of the size usually reserved for declarations of war or a moon landing—the headline read: GONNA HAVE SOME FUN TONIGHT.

Shelley spun back to see the counterman at the same

moment as he pulled his gaze away from the mutant dog to look at her. He was sweating profusely. Rivulets were pouring down his face from his brow.

"You're...you're sweating," Shelley said.

Because she had to say something. Because otherwise she might have to think about what was beginning to happen.

"Right," the counterman said. "Right. Sweating. Not good. Bad for business."

He took the folded towel from his arm and, pressing it tightly to his brow with both hands, wiped it down thoroughly in a single sweeping gesture.

His whole face went with it.

Every facial feature was wiped away, rubbed off in that one smooth slide of the towel as if they had been nothing more than stage make-up. What was left behind was neither a death's-head skull nor a bloodied slab of flesh and muscle, which fuck knows would have been bad enough, but was instead something arguably worse. A convex flesh-colored oval without eyes, ears, nose, or mouth.

Dropping the towel, the counterman's hands reached out searchingly toward where Shelley was sitting as if he hadn't yet realized the full horror of what had just happened to him and was trying to take hold of the last thing he had seen in hope of some clarification. Shelley threw herself off the stool and began to back away from the counter. Only when she'd put sufficient distance between her and the effaced travesty behind it did she look around at the rest of the coffee shop to see what else might be happening there.

Nothing was happening there, nor ever would again. Nothing *could* happen there, Shelley now saw, because the entire coffee shop was nothing but a painted stage set.

Everything that she'd previously seen as reality—the fixtures, the fittings, the food, even the customers—were just well-rendered paintings on four very large theatrical flats.

"What's happening?" Shelley shouted, unable to help herself from doing it even though she had no idea who she was asking and a horribly precise idea about who was listening.

As if her scream was a cue to some unseen stagehands, the painted flats flew violently apart from each other and fell noisily backward on the ground and Shelley was suddenly and completely alone in a vast and featureless black space.

But she was neither alone and nor was the space featureless for long. With a theatrical hiss of ignition, a spotlight flared into sudden life overhead and fixed her in its focused dazzle. Shelley jerked her head down, squinting instinctively against the light's initial blinding glare, and saw that her feet were planted on the painted black boards of what she was already realizing was a stage. Putting a shielding hand above her eyes and blinking through the spotlight's brightness, she looked out directly ahead of her.

Below and beyond the lip of the stage, arrayed in row after row of old-fashioned vaudeville seats, there was a whole audience looking back at her, an audience that consisted entirely of ventriloquist's dummies.

Male and female mixed, and most of them in old-school evening dress like they'd showed up to an open call for a slot on Ed Sullivan in 1957, the dummies were just sitting there—like you'd think dummies should—completely stationary.

Except for the ones who were moving.

Several of the small wooden things were in excited motion—twisting their plaster heads around to check out their peers, clacking their hinged jaws in eerily silent chatter, and, in one or two disturbing cases, pointing their painted fingers up at Shelley, their carved faces frozen yet somehow managing to look both amused and expectant.

In the third row, one of the dummies rose stiffly to its feet. Even through the dazzle of the spotlight Shelley could make out enough of its rough-hewn face to see that it had been made to look like a grotesque parody of Alex Drayton. Its arm jerked upwards gracelessly as if an invisible string had been carelessly pulled. Stabbing its pre-pointed finger in her direction, its artificial eyes rolling in their carved sockets to lock on hers and its jaw opening and snapping shut in approximate time with the words that came impossibly out of its mouth, the Drayton dummy shouted up at her.

"Thought she could just close her eyes!" it said, in a tone of disbelieving ridicule that anyone could ever be so naïve as that.

It began to laugh at her and, while its laughter was still taunting her and delighting the other dummies, another of the things, this one female, creaked its awkward and hideous way upright in the middle of the fifth row.

It was a cruel and lifeless caricature of Jen. A small yellow T-shirt was pulled snugly over her wooden and plaster chest and the slogan on it, stretched spring-break tight over her ludicrously handmade and horribly torpedo-sharp breasts, said *read 'em and weep*.

The Jen dummy pointed at Shelley too. "Forgot it was scarier in the dark!" it said.

A massive laugh track, like something from a particularly desperate sitcom, echoed throughout the auditorium, all the dummies' wooden mouths click-clacking in time with it.

The spotlight dimmed, to be replaced by old-fashioned footlights swelling into life at the foot of the stage. Their more diffuse light allowed Shelley to see her stage more clearly. Heavy red velvet curtains framed the proscenium and, over to the stage's far side, there was an easel of the type that, back in the golden days of music hall, used to hold placards announcing the name of each act.

From the darkness of the wings, two figures emerged, one of them holding such a placard. While his partner propped the card in place on the easel, Mister Sponge gave a grinning thumbs-up to Shelley and, once he was satisfied that the card was properly in position, Mister Scrotum turned to look at her as well. He winked at her knowingly and said, in a hoarse stage-whisper, "The show must go on," before following his smaller colleague off into the backstage shadows.

Shelley, still held helplessly in place by a paralyzing and overwhelming dread, looked at the placard. It read:

THE MOONGLOW SUPPER ROOM
PROUDLY PRESENTS
PROFESSOR ECHO.
MAGICIAN, VENTRILOQUIST.

"Pick a card," said a hideously familiar voice from immediately behind her and Shelley felt her body spasm in shock. She turned, slowly and reluctantly, to see who had joined her on the stage.

Dressed in full tuxedo with tails and wearing a top hat at an angle so jaunty as to practically defy gravity, Professor Echo was standing right beside her.

Moontown

Despite his shiny new outfit, Shelley had no trouble recognizing the monster's face. He was treating her to a delighted smile and was leaning in toward her, proffering in one extended hand the pack of trading cards which, with an effortless and professional thumb-flick, he spread out into a widely fanned arc.

"Any card," he continued.

Shelley didn't take a card. Didn't move at all. Wasn't even sure that she could.

Professor Echo gave her an understanding and sympathetic look. "Stage fright?" he said. "I understand. Allow me to help."

With a quick magician's flourish, the quickness of his terrible hand deceiving her terrified eye, the pack suddenly became one single card held upright between his thumb and forefinger, its back to Shelley his Beautiful Assistant. He was obviously using a house pack because Shelley recognized the design on the back of the card, knew its yellow base, deco graphics, and Streamline Moderne lettering with its jazz-age promise of cocktails and dancing.

Professor Echo didn't turn the card face out to show it to her, but instead just took a good close look at it himself. He nodded approvingly as he saw it. "Good choice," he said, the ghost of a smile hovering on his mouth.

He looked back at Shelley, all trace of a smile wiped clean, and raised a theatrical eyebrow.

"Game on," he said.

26

As soon as the professor had finished speaking, Shelley was somewhere else.

She'd experienced no sense of movement, had had no sense of distance covered or of time passing. It was more like she'd remained precisely in place while, in the blink of an eye, the entire world had changed around her.

She might have had no idea how she got there, but Shelley was unfortunately in no doubt as to where precisely she was. She was standing in the central aisle of King Shadow's nightmare church, the place that she had first seen in Tom Lawson's tortured memory. But the original source of the place wasn't what was important. All that mattered was that she was here now and that she knew, though she appeared to be alone at the moment, that something was either waiting for her or would soon come to claim her.

The church was lit only by occasional candles, big ones, high and wide and spiked in place atop four-feet-tall free-standing medieval style metal holders. Otherwise, the church was a thing of shadows, of great lakes of darkness between the few islands of light, treacherous spaces where anything or anyone could hide....

She'd arrived—or been set down, however the hell it worked—deep down along the central aisle, past most of the pews, much closer to the altar than to the front doors. But if she was going to move, she knew damned well in which direction she was going to be heading. No matter how many deep pools of dark shadow might hover menacingly between her and the exit, she still felt it was better to risk passing all of them than to move toward the altar space and put herself in the proximity of its perverse and blasphemous collection of crucifixes and their lunatic-eyed parodies of the Christ.

Shelley began a slow and cautious walk up the aisle toward the front doors. As she moved past the misshapen windows that she had seen before, she risked a look up at them and at the stained-glass eyes of the tortured saints portrayed upon them. Their eyes were hardly visible in the current darkness of the church, but they were just visible enough to allow her to see them shifting eerily to the side to watch her as she walked.

She could smell the perfumed and waxy aromas coming from the candles. The scents were far from unpleasant but Shelley's heart sank at the very fact of their presence. That she could smell them at all was not a good thing. She'd spent enough time in dreams, both her own and other people's, to know that for the most part the only senses that were really engaged in them were those of sight and of hearing. The fact that she could smell the candles, like the fact that she could fully feel every footstep she made up the aisle and was fully aware of how her clothes were sticking to the cold sweat of her frightened flesh, was an awful and ominous indicator of just how deeply the monster had her within his dominion, of just how thoroughly she was imprisoned within his version of reality.

As if sensing just where her mind was going, as if waiting for her to be hit by that revelation of how deeply she was immersed in his world, as if choosing that moment to let her see for how little the caution and silence of her walk up the aisle counted, the front doors of the church swung open as if pushed by nothing more than the force of his will, and King Shadow was revealed, standing framed in the moonlit doorway with his black robes swirling around him as if they carried their own winds.

It was overly theatrical, Shelley might have wasted time thinking, had she not been too busy feeling its melodrama work on her anyway, feeling herself all but ready to freeze like some hapless forest thing trapped by the cobra's mesmerizing dance. His eyes, almost as hooded now as those of a snake, were locked on hers—as if he too felt the metaphor and believed her to be incapable of movement—but she found the strength to force herself to look away, to look behind her back down the aisle for any other possible exit.

There were the pews and the alcoves, there were the spiral staircases, there was the choir gallery and the nave and the altar. There were the misshapen saints and the monstrous crucifixes. What there *wasn't* was any apparent way out.

King Shadow was patient. He let her take a good long look. As if there were rules of engagement to the sport of terrifying people, he waited till Shelley looked back at him before he took his first steps inside. After he'd covered a yard or so, the doors, again without being physically touched, slammed shut behind him.

In the tiny part of her brain that was still capable of objective judgment, Shelley found herself thinking that it was no wonder he liked to play with children because he was practically a fucking child himself, at least when it came to his sense of drama. The whole *look Ma, no hands* thing with the doors was like something an eleven-year-old would think was really impressive.

Moontown

Problem was, she thought, fear makes eleven-year-olds of all of us. Everything he was doing, no matter her rational mind's snotty opinion of it, was absolutely working on her. He was reducing her to a frightened child. Which was just how the bastard liked his women. Or his men. Fucker wasn't fussy.

Enough thinking. Time to run. Letting her watch his initial slow walk into the church was just about as much slack as she could count on being given, Shelley figured, so she spun back around and began hurtling down the aisle away from him, promising herself that she wouldn't look back unless she absolutely had to.

The chase began, and Shelley's promise to herself lasted about three seconds. It wasn't that she heard his steps become faster behind her, wasn't that she heard him gaining on her, melodrama and elegance be damned, it was that she suddenly couldn't hear him at all. Without slackening her speed, she looked back over her shoulder.

King Shadow had already halved the distance between them.

He was moving—like the Ragman had moved in Anthony's memory, like she assumed *all* of his selves could move—with a terrible and unnatural swiftness, like something flying without actually leaving the ground, like a speed skater jetting across invisible ice.

Shelley desperately tried to increase her own speed, driving herself forward toward the nave and, beyond it, the altar space, but before she turned her head back to face front again she saw something even more disheartening. Apparently his supernatural speed was not King Shadow's only trick. As Shelley watched, he passed into one of the pools of deep shadow and seemed to vanish inside it completely....

Not even knowing why she did it, Shelley snapped her head forward instantly—just in time to see the monster re-emerge from a *different* pool of shadow, this one directly in front of her.

Shelley, not screaming only because the shock was too deep and too sudden and she needed all her breath for running, stopped on a dime as the black-robed thing lunged for her. Purely on instinct, she threw herself to one side, evading his grasping arms by inches, and began running down the walkway of one of the long pews.

Directly ahead of her, on the floor of the walkway just a few feet from where the pew would let her out to a side aisle, there was a small circular pool of shadow. Surely that wasn't a problem? Surely he couldn't...?

Yes, he could.

Rising up from the narrow patch of darkness like a sea creature somehow breaking surface in a rock pool, King Shadow was once again in front of her.

This time she did scream. But she didn't stop moving. Diving into a sideways hurdle, she flung herself over the pew and, righting herself precariously, started racing again toward the front of the church.

King Shadow hadn't even tried to grab her that time, she realized, and—watching now as he vanished and reappeared time after effortless time, looming menacingly and instantaneously from various areas of the darknesses around her, both near to her running self and contemptuously far from it —she knew that he was simply toying with her, that this had become more a gleeful demonstration of his power than an immediate threat. He was enjoying himself, enjoying the whole process, taking his damned time about it, like he could just keep fucking with her until he was good and ready for the next stage of the game to begin.

Even if he wasn't trying to take actual hold of her yet, she could sense that his movements weren't completely arbitrary, could tell that he was *herding* her, limiting her choices of movement to the direction he needed her to go. Which was why she was soon on the raised wooden platform area close to the dressed altar.

Several of the oversized candles on their tall spiked holders burned brightly in the altar space's immediate area, but between and around all of them were several of the supernatural pools of darkness, and it was of course from these that King Shadow began to burst forth.

First here. Then there. Everywhere and anywhere. Into the darkness and out of it. Bastard was a one man circling operation. Single-handedly, he had Shelley surrounded—emerging from, and sinking back into, the darkness at will.

As if it no longer mattered that she saw it, as if in fact it merely added the spice of frustrated hope to her cocktail of terror and confusion, being forced up into this area allowed Shelley to see that there was another door beyond the altar-area, perhaps just a door to an alcove or a robing area, or perhaps an exit. But in any case, she was separated from it by another of the pools of shadow, a big one, one that attempting to cross would almost certainly deliver her directly into the surfacing arms of the monster.

Shelley looked back from the door to King Shadow, still playing with her, still taunting her, still sliding effortlessly in to and out of various areas of the darknesses, keeping her trapped within the circles of candles and shadow around the altar.

She let him take his next showman's dive into one of the shadow pools, using the brief second of his disappearance to test something. She grabbed up one of the tall candleholders and, holding it lengthwise out in front of her, swept the candle's light in the direction of the bigger pool of darkness by the door.

The shadow shrank back from the light.

So, whatever their magical nature that allowed their master his entry and exit privileges, the shadows were still fucking *shadows*. If light shone on them, they could be driven back. Good to know.

Yeah, good to know. But so the hell what? Because King Shadow was already stepping out of another of the shadow pools around the altar. The speed at which he came and went simply wasn't going to allow her to gain any distance through any shadow she might manage to temporarily clear.

Besides, he'd stopped the routine.

He was still where he'd last surfaced, just a couple of yards from Shelley, and was simply standing there. His hooded eyes took in the candleholder in her hands as if he saw instantly not only what she'd been doing in the tiny moment of his absence but what she'd been thinking and hoping to do.

He grinned. Or showed her his teeth. Jury was still out.

"Ah," he said in mock solemnity. "A candle in the darkness…"

Shelley looked at him, scared but defiant, still hoisting her candleholder.

He was done with the herding and the swan dive showing off, she saw. He was done with the teasing. Like any asshole fucking bully, he knew that once a victim stops running and does something else, *anything* else, even as simple an act as pointing a candle at a shadow, it was time to remind them who was boss, to move from screwing with their mind to hurting them properly.

He began walking toward her now, slowly and implacably.

"A candle in the darkness," he repeated. "But I *am* the darkness."

He was very close to her now, so very close. Close enough to reach out and touch her...

One last little flourish proved irresistible, though.

As when he had first appeared in the doorway and gone all *Night on Bald Mountain* on her, his black winglike robes began to billow up and out, whipping around him as if riding invisible winds.

It was as impressive as before, and even more frightening because of the proximity. But it allowed Shelley one vital second to think, to remember how the shadow on the floor had flinched from the candle's light, how magical shadows were still *physical* shadows.

If shadows were shadows, robes were robes.

She suddenly thrust the candle directly at him like a flame-headed spear.

"Let there be light," she said, 'cause who gave *him* the fucking monopoly on dumb-ass one-liners?

The flame ignited his flowing black robes instantly, like they were so much tissue paper, and fire began to race all over King Shadow's form.

Shelley knew better than to take any time at all to enjoy it. Pulling the candleholder away, she took a half-step back— partly because the fire was suddenly so big and powerful and, you know, fucking *hot*—and partly so that she could do what came next. Taking an even firmer grip on the candleholder, she slammed it violently down at a sharp angle on the floor, knocking the candle from its perch and revealing the thick four-inch-long spike on which it had been skewered.

Both hands on the haft of the candleholder, Shelley thrust it forcefully downward like a harpoon, spearing it right through one of King Shadow's feet and into the wooden floor of the platform, trapping the monster in place as the flames continued to consume him.

Now she could take a second.

She kept looking at him, a wise couple of yards back beyond the reach of his writhing and blistering arms, until - finally, satisfyingly—he screamed, his face a ruined melting mask and his body little more than a furious pillar of flame.

Only when the scream stopped, only when there was no tongue or larynx left with which the monster *could* scream, did she turn away, cross to the side door and exit through it.

Did she actually *hear* the sound of a card being flipped, as if somewhere Professor Echo was still running through his magic act, or was that just how her mind chose to make sense of what happened next?

Because as she went through the door—the second she stepped out of it rather—there *was* no door. She was neither still in the church nor outside of it. She was instead standing just above a sandbox on one of the rises in the moonlit playground of the garden of delights, having been moved there as simply and as instantaneously as when she'd been placed in the church.

Needless to say, she wasn't alone.

Very close to her, the little dead siblings, the pale brother and sister, were sitting cross-legged on the moon-silvered grass, and their blank and lifeless eyes were fixed on the black-clad storyteller who was sitting on a chair in front of them.

Jimmy Midnight's unnaturally long legs were stretched out in front of him, crossed as awkwardly and as unsettlingly as if a long-legged spider were making a stab at human posture. He had what looked like a big oversized children's storybook on his lap. With its thick leather binding, ribbed spine hubs, and flaking gilt design work, the book seemed very old, as if Jimmy or someone very like him might have been reading from the same volume for centuries.

Given her visit, Shelley was surprised that he hadn't chosen to read from her old pal Wilfred Tibble's little yellow-jacketed masterpiece *Jenny and the Dark*—because this whole place seemed to be real big on the fucking in-jokes—but she stood and listened anyway as, running his finger down the text of the last page, he wrapped up the story that he had been reading to the children.

"…and just when all seemed lost," he said, his voice a sing-song mockery of old fashioned schoolmarm diction, "the brave hero took up his sword and, swinging it with all his strength and hoping with all his heart, he cut off the head of the Hydra."

Jimmy slammed the book shut and leaned his head sinuously forward—as with the disturbingly crossed legs, it was as if the articulation of the neck muscles remembered belonging to an anatomy other than the human—in order that his black as coal eyes could look directly at the dead brother and sister.

"Stupid little fuck," he said. "The Hydra just grew more heads and ripped him to bloody tatters."

Leaving the lesson to sink in on his silent and captive audience, Jimmy looked over at Shelley. "Is the moral completely clear, do you think?" he said. "Or shall you and I demonstrate it pragmatically for the little darlings?"

He threw the book carelessly over his shoulder and stood up. He was every bit as tall as Taylor Smith had said he was. He made no actual move toward her—not yet—but Shelley was already beginning to back away down the grassy rise.

Jimmy raised his arms in front of him, bent at the elbows with the forearms upright, the backs of his hands toward Shelley.

"Oh, how my garden grows..." he said, like he was quoting from something else to be found in his big black book of lessons.

Each of his fingernails grew eerily upward until they were more than six inches long. Keeping his jet-black eyes on Shelley, he turned his hands proudly and slowly in the moonlight for her to see how the nails glinted like freshly sharpened razors.

He still hadn't actually moved toward her yet, and all the movements he had made had been leisurely and slow. Until he jabbed his razor nails through the air with a terrifying suddenness.

"BOO!" he shouted.

The glinting points of the nails came to a quivering stop just half a taunting inch from Shelley's face. The speed was almost as impressive as the precision. Shelley hadn't even had time to move. But she moved now, turning and running down the rise before he could decide that teasing was okay as far as it went but wasn't nearly as much fun as stabbing and ripping.

She heard no sound of pursuit, just Jimmy's delighted laughter echoing behind her...

...as once again she found she wasn't where she had been.

Moontown

Instead, still running—and she doubted she'd have reason to stop anytime soon—she was smack in the middle of the shadowy central aisle of the first place she had ever seen here, back before she knew that there really *was* a here, the huge derelict garment factory from Anthony's tormented memory.

Her racing feet were carrying her past the giant industrial sewing machines and the towering bales of fabric. Just as Anthony had done, Shelley looked back behind her and saw, just as Anthony had seen, that the far end of the room was being swallowed up by a sentient darkness in motion and that, within that darkness, the Ragman was heading her way.

Instinctively, like the rabbit who knows the hound has just seen it, Shelley swerved to her side, not slackening her pace but beginning to weave in and out of the intersecting machine-packed aisles that ran the entire length of the main factory floor, as if hoping that keeping herself out of his direct sight might somehow slow the monster down.

The Ragman was moving straight ahead but he wasn't yet moving as fast as Shelley knew that he could. It was more like he was surfing, riding the wave of the darkness, letting it carry him forward until he felt that it was time to put her out of her misery. Shelley could sense—almost smell—his horrible confidence, his power and his eagerness. Like it didn't matter where she went or how fast she ran. Like there was only ever one possible outcome to this chase.

Through the high windows that ran down the side wall of the factory Shelley could see not only the lonely main street of Moontown itself—she wasn't actually sure that that jibed with the geography as she'd seen it when she was on the street earlier but figured that city planning was as fluid and protean here as everything else seemed to be—but also the whole nightmare landscape of dark hills and lost highways that surrounded it and, holding sway over all, the huge and bright moon shining its cold silver-blue light down on its dream territory.

As she darted down a side aisle alongside another of the big industrial machines, her eyes took in its metal bedplates and its vast insectlike needle-housings, waiting to be fed by the still-in-place huge cotton reels. She also realized, perhaps a little late, that her running feet were echoing out noisily as they pounded their way across the old stone floor.

"I hear you," the Ragman said, like it was all a jolly game of hide-and-seek. His voice sounded at once far away and right inside her head.

So he could hear her. Well, she could hear him too. Hear him as he jumped into place at the head of the side aisle, hear his expectant inhalation as he prepared to savor her scream at the sudden sight of him, hear his disappointed sigh at the fact that she was no longer in the aisle. Sorry, Charlie. Scared, not stupid.

She'd rounded the corner the second she realized he could hear her feet, but not before making sure he wouldn't hear them again. She'd kicked three of the big machines into life and now the busy and deafening clatter of their rapidly pistoning heads were drowning out any other sounds, echoing throughout the entire room as their needle noses slammed furiously and repeatedly into the bedplates, cotton trailing out wildly from them.

From where she was crouched carefully and quietly behind another machine in a neighboring aisle, one that ran at right angles to the first and crossed the factory widthwise instead of lengthwise, Shelley watched the angry disappointment flare in the monster's eyes. It was only there for a moment, though, and was soon replaced by what presumably passed for a smile in the kingdom of the cruel.

He moved slowly and patiently down the first aisle, killing each machine in turn and listening to their chittering sounds running down to silence. When he spoke again, his voice was quiet and intimate, very confident that she was nearby and listening. "Teasing me," he said. "Oh, I *like* that in a victim."

At the sound of a creak from somewhere else within the maze of aisles—well, okay, from right beneath her fucking elbow as it leaned too trustingly on a support bar beneath a reel housing—the Ragman's head jerked to the side as if trying to locate the sound. Shelley was sure that he was probably about to smile again, but she wasn't looking at him anymore. Instead, she was inching her way down the other aisle, keeping low and moving cautiously, trying for silence.

Ahead of her, past several more machines, at the end of the widthwise aisle there was a narrow side walkway that ran lengthwise directly alongside one of the factory walls. Shelley made her crouching way toward it, feeling her way ahead mostly with her hands, saving her eyes to keep looking back over her nervous shoulder to be sure that the Ragman hadn't quietly stepped into place right behind her. Because she knew damned well that that was exactly the kind of shit he'd get a big kick out of pulling.

As she reached the last machine and the end of the aisle, she took a final look behind her and then moved out into the walkway, only to see that there was a figure directly in front of her.

She really didn't know how she'd managed to stifle the scream because it took her frightened and confused eyes a full second to register that the figure, semi-sprawled against the bare brick of the factory wall below one of the high windows, was merely one of those life-size rag dolls that she'd seen with Anthony.

She thought about taking a moment to punch it in the fucking face for nearly stopping her heart but she was too interested in what she'd seen at the far end of the walkway to bother. There was a door there. It was an old-fashioned connecting door, the upper half of which was filled by a large panel of smoked glass, which meant she couldn't see where the door led, but if she could reach it she could go through it —even if it meant smashing the frickin' window if the door itself was locked—and what was the alternative? Keep playing frightened mouse to the Ragman's tireless cat? Hell with that. Still keeping low, Shelley stepped carefully over the splayed legs of the rag doll and started down the walkway.

His timing was impeccable, she'd give the bastard that. Because almost as soon as she started moving in its direction, the eerily elongated shadow of the Ragman fell across the smoked glass door. He was heading to the walkway down the last aisle, the one immediately before the door.

She was still a couple of yards from the next nearest aisle where she could take cover. She was terrified that he'd step into the walkway before she could reach it, but she had to try. Speeding up as much as she could without making any giveaway noise, she just managed to turn into the aisle and crouch behind the shelter of its last machine in time.

Through the camouflaging lattice of the machine's legs and strut supports, she saw the Ragman move into the narrow walkway, pause there, and look along it.

She knew that he couldn't see her. But she could tell that

he could sense her closeness. He sniffed the air showily, as if he knew that she was watching him.

"Mmm," he said, with the anticipation of a gourmet diner who'd just breathed in the aroma of his next meal. "I can smell your fear, Shelley." He paused. "Or is that perhaps excitement?"

He began moving up the walkway, slowly and deliberately, passing aisle after successive aisle, his eyes flicking sideways to take a cursory glance along each one, as if he knew that one of them would soon reveal her to him.

Shelley, still crouching low behind her machine, looked up at the hand she was using to steady herself in position, its clinging fingertips resting on the edge of the machine near its needle bed.

She needed to get him into a parallel aisle, get him distracted, needed room to get herself some options instead of just waiting here to be delivered into his hands. There was a rusted screw already halfway out of its housing in one of the thin cross-supports that ran between the big legs of the machine. Could she...?

She reached out to the screw and gave it the most tentative of turns, very aware that the slightest noise could drive the Ragman from his slow teasing walk into the nightmare speed of which she knew him to be capable.

The screw moved.

The screw didn't squeak.

She loved that screw like she'd never loved a boyfriend.

Forcing herself not to hurry—even though every slow turn of the screw and each passing second brought the monster aisle by aisle, step by step, inch by inch closer to her—she worked the rusted thing fully loose from its hole.

Rolling it between her thumb and forefinger to build up some traction and get a good controlling grip on it, Shelley crouched even lower to stare through the busy obstacle course of overlaid and interconnecting struts and supports beneath the machine, trying to find a clear through route for her beautiful rusted distraction.

The Ragman was just two aisles away from her now. She was just going to have to go for it. She waited until he was just about clear of the aisle before last and then, blessing it and wishing it luck, she flicked the screw forward. It sailed effortlessly below her machine, avoiding every obstacle and then—like it did this for a fucking living and what was she so worried about?—pinged gloriously loud against the leg of a machine in the next aisle over.

The Ragman—who for one fabulous deluding second Shelley could think of as just another born sucker—went right for it. As the sound rang out, he didn't just glance into the aisle the way he'd been doing with the others but rushed into it and raced headlong down it, his hideously eager eyes scanning every machine there for hiding places.

But he didn't look long.

As if sensing he'd been played the Ragman suddenly froze, turned, and looked back to stare directly over at the machine from behind which Shelley had flicked the screw.

And she knew then, by the small merciless smile that played on his face, that he'd seen them, knew that, despite the dimness of the moonlight, the Ragman had caught sight of the tiny edges of the fingers that were resting on the far side of the machine.

He was back up the parallel aisle in less than a second, moving with that silent and eerie sliding motion of his until he was on the other side of the machine. His eyes glittering with dark joy, he leaned forward, swiftly but still quietly, and then with a tight little sigh of pleasure he jetted his arm across the bed of the machine to grab the fingers of the hiding hand.

As he started to yank up the hand he'd taken hold of—the hand of the rag doll that Shelley had grabbed from the walkway in the precious seconds he'd spent heading down the other aisle—Shelley leapt out from the walkway behind the head of the machine and slammed her own hand down on the start button and, with a deafening clatter, the head plunged its industrial-strength needle into the Ragman's forearm.

Shelley guessed the needle's rate as about twenty stabs a second, but who was counting? Not her. All she cared about was that the monster's arm was trapped in place as the needle punched its unspooling cotton endlessly into his flesh.

Shelley knew better than to wait around to enjoy the sight. She was off and running almost immediately, hurtling down the walkway toward the door. But that first second's image was burned in her brain, that moment when she'd seen the Ragman's face twisted in pain and seen blood—*blood!*—pour from his trapped arm as the huge machine head continued to drive the needle into him.

She heard his roar of rage behind her and then the sound of the machine juddering into a new kind of chaos. One glance over her shoulder let her see that he was forcefully dragging his arm back across the bed-plate, the needle continuing to burrow stitches into his flesh all the way, spattering both the machine and the monster with blood.

She didn't wait to see him finally yank his hand clear, though the tiny part of her mind that still had room for the ridiculous took a moment to wonder if the needle would finish its work off with a nice locked filigree pattern between whichever of his fingers were the last to come free. Yeah well, tied with a pretty bow or not, she knew he'd be turning to give chase again any second so she put her mind back to racing feverishly toward the door.

Her hand grasped the handle, and of course it didn't turn. The door was locked. She rattled at the handle furiously again, which was pretty fucking stupid because locked is locked. She looked back behind her. The Ragman was all but free of the machine and, once he was, she didn't think he'd be in any mind to dawdle.

Desperately, she scanned the immediate area. There was a metal wastebasket by the last of the machines, full of cloth off-cuts and discards. She grabbed it, tipped out the contents, raised it to shoulder height, and smashed out the glass panel in the upper half of the door.

Behind her, she saw that the monster had not only cleared his arm from the machine but had already covered more than half of the walkway and was almost upon her.

She turned and flung the metal wastebasket at the Ragman. It reached him alright, but he smashed it aside with an effortless sweep of his arm and it didn't slow him down at all.

With no time to think about whether she could do it or not, Shelley ran at the door and launched herself into an arcing dive through the shattered panel, tumbling into a braking roll on the other side of the door. Jeez. Maybe she could have been a cheerleader after all. She straightened up and saw where she was.

"Fuck," she said.

Moontown

The door led only to a stairwell. There was nothing ahead of her but a staircase leading upward. She looked up the stairwell. No good news. Just five or six flights of stairs connected by narrow landings leading all the way up to a roof exit.

But beggars can't be choosers. Behind her, the door was already splintering into pieces under the Ragman's violent assault and he was nearly through into the stairwell. Shelley started up the stairs, three steps at a time, reaching the first landing almost without thinking about it. Starting up the next flight allowed her the dubious luxury of looking back down the central shaft to see that the Ragman had entered the stairwell.

He looked up, smiling. He began to climb the stairs after her, back to patient and slow mode. Like there was no rush. Like he knew she had no way out.

Logically, Shelley knew that if he wasn't rushing then she probably had no need to either. But try telling that to a racing heart and a terrified mind. As far as they were concerned, logic could go fuck itself. She was rushing. Because every alarm bell in her nervous system was telling her she had to. She pounded up the stairs, forcing herself around each corner, up each flight, until she reached the final landing at the top of the stairwell and slammed her way through the exit door to emerge onto the roof of the factory, open to the night sky and bathed in the ubiquitous moonlight.

Shelley could stop running now. Because there was nowhere to run and there was nowhere to hide.

The roof was wide and flat. Running around the edges there was a low perimeter wall, a two-foot-high lip-service nod to safety that wouldn't ever actually have prevented anyone from falling or jumping to the streets and alleys below, should either dizziness or despair have prompted them to it. The roof was otherwise empty, apart from a few randomly scattered vents and chimneys, and its biggest feature, in fact, was the slant-roofed doorway from which she'd just emerged.

And from which, quite soon now, the Ragman would come to take her.

Shelley ran over to the perimeter wall, looking down to see if there was anywhere or anything to which it was possible to jump. But there was nothing between her and the cold hard ground more than a hundred feet below.

"Don't fall," said a voice from not far behind her. "That would spoil all the fun."

Shelley turned around slowly.

The Ragman, having just emerged from the stairwell, was heading across the roof towards her. Shelley didn't move. There was finally nowhere to move to. She just stood and waited as the monster closed the distance between them.

She didn't want to meet his eyes until she had to. She looked up for a moment. Overhead, the heavy moon was shining down on its terrible kingdom, razor-thin traces of shadow creeping across its surface like ripples of intent.

The Ragman had stopped about three feet from her. Shelley, very aware of how close she still was to the low perimeter wall and the precipitous drop beyond it, finally lowered her eyes and looked directly into his face.

"Why wasn't it over?" she asked him. "Why couldn't I just forget you?"

The Ragman managed to look both incredulous and insulted. "Because I'm un-fucking-forgettable!" he snapped at her. "What? You think you have a *choice* here?"

Shelley had another question. "You... *this* you, I mean...

you were *Anthony's* fear," she said. "And King Shadow—he was Tom Lawson's. But they're *dead*, both of them. Why are you still...?"

The Ragman cut her off. "I don't belong to *them*, you stupid little girl," he said. "They belong to *me*!" And then he laughed in delighted triumph and took a long look up at the moon before shouting out for not just her to hear, "*I am infinite!*"

As his eyes returned to her face, Shelley could think of nothing whatever to say or do. He was infinite. She felt defeat eating its way through her.

As he'd done earlier, the Ragman breathed in and sighed, as if tasting a gourmet delicacy or sipping a fine wine. "I can see the light dying in your eyes," he said. "I can taste the hope decaying in you, smell the despair. It's all so... *sweet*."

He paused, for quite a long time. Making sure to let it all really sink into her, let it take a good firm hold. "Now come here," he said. "And let me hurt you."

Shelley didn't move. Not immediately. But she knew that he could see that there was no fight left in her. She looked down, as if afraid to meet his eyes.

"Don't worry," he said. "I'll never take it *too* far. You're my ride, Shelley. My ticket to the world. To all the others..."

Shelley snapped her head up and looked directly at him.

"Then I *do* have a choice," she said.

And she stepped off the roof.

The Ragman leapt forward, leaning out over the perimeter and flinging his arm out to snatch at Shelley, who grabbed his wrist and, using his forward momentum as leverage against him, simultaneously spun herself back—to let her other hand grab a precarious hold on the tip of the perimeter wall—

and yanked him forward and down, tipping him over the edge. Her clutching fingers ripped at the rags that formed the flesh of his wrist, keeping hold of one strand of material…

…so that, as the Ragman fell, he literally *unraveled*, his humanoid form ribboning apart into a long streaming spiral of thin multicolored cloth.

Only when he had come completely undone did she let go of the cloth and get her other hand onto the rim of the perimeter wall. She pulled herself up, straining with effort—yeah, thanks for bogarting that whole upper-body-strength thing, guys—until she could finally get one elbow over the wall and start to clamber back over it onto the roof.

She stood. And the second she did…

…she realized that she was standing not in the open air of the rooftop but back in the main room of the Funhouse.

The flickering string lights gave their dim illumination to the eerie and deserted space as, behind her, the carousel with its nightmare horses began creaking to a halt as if the night's last ride was over.

But it wasn't.

There were noises in the shadows—here, there, everywhere—and blurred movements at the edges of her vision, movements that refused to become concrete and real no matter how Shelley spun around to try and keep track of them.

The noises, though, became a little clearer. They were a million tiny whispers, like the distant and disembodied voices of lost children rustling like dry leaves in the darkness and echoing around the empty space. All of them were saying the same thing, but the voices were phasing in and out of sync with each other, making it hard for Shelley to understand them. Only as she finally managed to make out what it was they were saying—*Johnny in the Dark, Johnny in the Dark, Johnny in the Dark*—did the carousel judder to a final stillness.

A figure was sitting sidesaddle on one of the monstrous horses. With an effortless slide, he dismounted and stood on the carousel's red painted wooden platform to stand facing Shelley.

There was nothing glamorous or theatrical about this one. No black-wing robes or coat of many colors, no stovepipe hat or spider-stilt legs. But then, there never had been. Shelley's childhood terrors hadn't run to the kind of widescreen and technicolor excess that the other avatars had enjoyed flaunting. Johnny in the Dark was a mean man in a long black coat. That was all. That was enough.

"Hi," he said. "I'm the one that doesn't fuck around, as you doubtless remember." His voice, too, seemed to prefer underplaying to chewing the scenery. It aimed for the kind of downbeat free-of-affect tone where the terminally hip meets the sociopathic. A couple of degrees warmer and it might have been cool. But it wasn't cool. It was chilling.

From an inside pocket of his long black coat, he produced an old-fashioned straight razor and flicked it open. Again, his movement was simple, almost off-handed. All the drama was in the blade, which glinted and shimmered with reflected light.

Shelley began backing away from the carousel.

Johnny stepped off the platform lightly and easily. His smile was light and easy too, the smile of a babysitter or a camp counselor, the smile of someone who knew how to smile at little girls in a way that would win a parent's affection. "Do you remember what I am, Shelley?" he said. "You do, don't you?"

Peter Atkins

He waited for a moment, as if actually expecting her to answer. When she didn't, when she just kept backing away from him, he didn't sound angry or disappointed. He sounded as if he was perfectly happy to provide the answer himself. "I'm everything that happens when all the lights go out."

And all the lights went out.

"Oh, look," he said in the dark. "There's our cue."

In the sudden impenetrable blackness, Shelley heard the sound of rushing feet and knew that he was coming for her.

There was a momentary glint of light as the razor slashed through the air in the place she'd last been standing. She wasn't standing there anymore, of course. She was running, helplessly in the dark, banging into things, stumbling, nearly falling. She knew that the glint of light from the razor made no sense. It was like a reflection, but there was no light in the placc to be reflected. Guess the bastard wasn't quite as free of his brothers' showmanship as his disaffected persona liked to pretend. As if to confirm that when the lights were down the mask was off, the next sound that echoed in the darkness, hot on the heels of another slash-of-light razor streak, was a lunatic giggle. Johnny was enjoying the game now, just like the others, and fuck the Joe Cool shit.

She kept *hitting* things in the dark. Hard things. Sharp things. Things with corners. Jesus. She was too adrenalized to feel any pain from whatever damage they might be doing to her, but every time she ran into something he *heard* her. And there'd be another slash of light as the razor streaked down. And another. And another. And each one getting closer to her than the one before as the giggling madman at her heels grew better at judging the distance.

She was already beginning to feel that she might be fleeing

his blade through this nightmare darkness forever when, some distance ahead of her, she finally saw a narrow band of light, tiny and at floor level. Was it a door? Was light escaping from an adjacent room beneath a door? She had no idea, she just knew she had to try for it. She also knew that if the band of light remained clear and unbroken in her eye-line then there could be no hard-sharp-things-with-corners between her and it.

Shelley had no idea what a beeline was—and c'mon, who the hell *did?*—but she figured that's what she was making as she raced for the band of light, arms already extended in front of her to slam open the door that she believed, trusted, prayed would be there....

And it was.

And, knocking it open and hardly slowing as she ran into the room beyond, she could suddenly see again. Could, in fact, see *herself* again. See many herselves again. The vast room was full of Shelley Campbells, hundreds of her, all running, all terrified.

As her eyes got over the initial illusion, she saw that, though the room itself was just another featureless square, a maze-like structure had been imposed upon it by the presence of literally hundreds of free-standing mirrors.

A hall of mirrors. Figured. No carnival complete without one.

Seconds later, Johnny in the Dark came through the door after her. He paused for a moment to take in their surroundings—"Nice," he said. "You can watch yourself bleed"—and then rushed at her again, swinging his razor and missing her by mere centimeters as she began running through the maze of mirrors.

She ran.

He chased.

The razor danced and threatened.

And the mirrors' endless reflections confused her horribly. Was that him directly ahead of her? Or was that a reflection of him behind her?

She turned corner after corner in the looking-glass labyrinth, seeing his pursuing reflection change angle behind her as she raced past mirror after mirror... until suddenly his reflection wasn't there anymore.

Shelley stopped, suspecting a trick, poised to run again.

She held her breath. Listened. She couldn't hear him.

Cautiously, she began moving forward quietly, feeling a different kind of tension now as she inched her slow way through the mirrors, knowing that at any second...

Slash!

The razor sliced down her forearm, quick hot and insistent, searing a long thin cut deep into her flesh, a cut so thin that it was almost invisible until the flowing blood defined it for her.

Johnny moved out from behind the mirror and watched her happily as she gasped in pain and cradled her wounded arm.

Shelley stepped backward away from him, eyes fixed on him as he moved toward her, weaving his razor through the air like a dancing snake.

Her foot bumped into something behind her and she turned around to look in the mirror that she'd hit. She saw herself as a child, saw her own eight-year-old eyes staring back at her in paralyzed terror.

And there it was, Shelley thought. There *she* was. Just

where she'd always been.

Swallowed by the dark.

Swallowed by the dark all those years ago and never really free. Everything else just a cruel mercy, the reaches of her life just the slack in the leash that bound her to the monster.

As if her own reflection was the key to understanding, every mirror in the room was suddenly filled by the image of a terrified child. A room full of trapped and frightened souls. All creeds, all colors. Shelley glanced feverishly around at reflection after reflection, so overwhelmingly appalled that she hardly noticed Johnny had stopped to take it all in too. Though of course it wasn't so new to him.

"Quite a collection, yes?" he said. "And new acquisitions arriving all the time..."

He didn't need to direct her attention. She saw immediately what he was referring to. In one of the mirrors she could see Taylor Smith in room seven of the Freeway Motel. He was sitting at the table and staring at what Shelley knew to be the wall mirror in the room, staring in startled fear as if something had just tapped at the other side of the glass to let him know it was there.

"Oh, you bastard..." Shelley said, half under her breath. Like there was a point to saying it aloud. Like he needed telling.

Johnny laughed at her.

"Welcome to your own fear, Shelley," he said. "The fear of your utter inability to help anyone. You're not going to save Taylor. You're not going to save anybody. What can you do? There're so many of them, and new recruits come every night. Every night. Every time they close their precious little eyes, I can find them. You can't help them. *You're one of them.*

How can you help others when you can't even help yourself?"

Shelley looked back at the mirror nearest to her, the one that contained her own child-reflection. She felt her face crumbling in defeat as she stared at the lost and frightened little girl, who suddenly sobbed as if at a fresh wave of despair, a tear starting down her cheek.

Shelley—instinctively, without thinking, without allowing her own fear to get in the way—raised her arm to comfort the child.

Her hand slipped effortlessly through the mirror to wipe the tear from the child's eye.

As if it was the most natural thing in the world, Shelley put both her arms forward, unhampered by doubt and ignoring the presence of the capering idiot with the razor, and pulled the little girl easily from the mirror, bringing her to her and cradling her in a warm embrace.

"Hush," she said. "Hush. There's nothing to be afraid of."

Over the burrowing head of the child, Shelley looked up and met the eyes of the monster. "*There's nothing to be afraid of,*" she said again.

She felt the child's body relax against her, returning the hug, and then she felt her fade away completely. And she knew, without needing to look, that every mirror in the place was suddenly empty.

He'd said he was unforgettable, and he'd been right. That was her mistake. It wasn't about forgetting. It was about remembering. It was about remembering all the other things that were just as true as whatever dark imaginings brought you to the vile attentions of this filthy night-haunting creature.

Johnny looked at his empty mirrors and then back at her.

Moontown

There was, big fucking surprise, an angry snarl on his face. But there was something else, too. There was doubt in his eyes.

"*'There's nothing to be afraid of,'*" he sneered. "I'll make sure they carve that on your headstone. Or your face."

He lifted his razor menacingly and moved towards her.

Shelley didn't flinch. "Fuck you," she said.

Every mirror in the place exploded, shattering into scores upon scores of jagged shards...

"My dream," said Shelley. "My rules."

...that flew into the air like the arrows of a thousand archers, every one of them jetting toward Johnny in the Dark. He tried to run; he tried to fight; he tried to swing his razor in defense, but it was useless. The jagged mirror blades swept and slashed at him from a hundred different directions, cutting, ripping, slicing, tearing...

Shelley watched, silent, unmoving, ecstatic, as her dream shards slashed the screaming monster to pieces.

And she meant *pieces*. Wretched tiny lumps of bloody flesh that only a sushi chef could do anything with.

Shelley stared at the steaming mess on the floor for quite a long time, stared until she was fully satisfied that the last twitching morsel was finally still.

Only then—very consciously, very precisely—did she close her eyes...

27

...and open them again on the bed in room seven.

Taylor, still sitting and watching the TV, looked over at her.

"Hi," said Shelley.

"Hi," Taylor replied.

Shelley glanced around the room briefly—she didn't believe the walls were going to be revealed as painted stage-flats but she didn't want to be taken by surprise either—and then looked back at Taylor.

"First time I've woken up, right?" she said.

"Right," said Taylor.

Shelley looked at the sunlight strong-arming its way through the pathetic motel curtains and allowed herself to breathe. Deeply, strongly, and slowly.

Midnight would always come and people would always dream. Shelley knew that. Knew too that midnight would stake its claim in some dreamers' hearts and the thing she had faced whisper itself back into existence. She knew that the moon would have its dominion and its misbegotten king, in whatever flesh it had freshly clothed itself, be remembered again.

But this dream, at least, was over. And she and the boy were awake and safe.

Taylor was still looking at her. Patient. Ready to see what came next.

"You okay?" she asked him.

Moontown

"Yeah," he said.
"Good."
She smiled at the boy.
The boy smiled back.

MAR 17 2009

WA

40.00
3.00

ATKINS

DATE DUE	
MAY 2 7 2009	
JUL 2 9 2009	
AUG 0 3 2009	
SEP 2 6 2009	
GAYLORD	PRINTED IN U.S.A.